A Taste of Temptation

Colin T. Nelson

Rumpole Press of Minneapolis

Copyright © 2016 Colin T. Nelson

ISBN-13: 9780692769195

All rights reserved

Dedication

Once again, to my wonderful wife, Pam.

Also by Colin T. Nelson

Reprisal
Fallout
Flashover
The Amygdala Hijack
Up Like Thunder

Acknowledgments

While writing these stories, I had tremendous help from several people: Marilyn Curtis, who is so good at reading and critiquing the rough drafts; my editor, Jennifer Adkins, who doesn't miss a period; and, of course, my toughest editor, greatest idea-generator, and loving wife, Pamela Nelson. My thanks also to Dr. Mitch Morey, Assistant Hennepin County Medical Examiner, for his insights into poisons and autopsies, and to TV chef Bobby Flay for permission to use one of his tasty recipes.

Thanks to all of you for your help and support.

When we get out of the glass bottle of our ego and when we escape like the squirrels in the cage of our personality and get into the forest again, we shall shiver with cold and fright. But things will happen to us so that we don't know ourselves. Cool, unlying life will rush in.

—D. H. Lawrence

Contents

Prospect Park

When my partner and I got the call that warm fall night, we thought it would be routine. Since I had recently been promoted to detective with the Minneapolis Police Department, I was paired with a senior detective for training. Dispatch told us only that there was a "victim down" in Prospect Park.

We made a U-turn and drove along University Avenue until we turned right on Franklin Avenue. Prospect Park was built early in the century (1900) to provide housing for the faculty from the University of Minnesota close by. The roads wrapped around the only hill in the city, capped by a small park at the top with an abandoned water tower. It had vacant open windows that resembled dead eyes, and over them was a black conical roof. For decades, everyone had called it the "witch's hat."

Detective Sonneson and I reached the crime scene at 10:36 p.m. We stopped at the St. Panteleimon Russian Orthodox church. It was a small white structure with an onion dome, a few gravestones, and a low iron fence that circled the grounds. The vic was inside the fence at the back of the church, hidden from the surrounding streetlights.

We exited our department vehicle and met the copper who'd first arrived at the scene.

"What've we got, son?" Detective Sonneson asked the officer.

"Middle-aged woman, face down, looks like she's been stabbed and maybe raped. She's dead, and I already sent for the medical boys." He detailed what he'd found at the scene so far. "It's a mess."

With a nod, I introduced myself. "Detective Luke Smith." Even though the word "detective" sounded odd coming out of my mouth, I felt proud but hoped it didn't show.

The air was still warm from an Indian summer day while dried leaves crackled around us from the gusting wind. Above, bare branches in the trees scraped against each other as if to warn us that winter was coming, or something worse. They couldn't have known it was my duty to investigate this crime.

Sonneson sighed and slipped on blue latex gloves. They snapped over his wrists. He picked his way through the dry grass to look at the body. I followed behind him. When he reached the vic, he said, "Let's be careful not to disturb anything and turn her over."

If there was some way I could've avoided helping my partner, I would have taken it. But then, fate had put me on duty that night in that place. We inched our gloved hands underneath the body and rolled it to the right.

Thankfully, I was kneeling, because otherwise, I probably would've fallen down. I knew the victim. Mackenzie Monroe. We'd gone to high school together, although we had moved in distinctly different circles. Even at thirty-nine, she was still temptingly beautiful. Her thick hair had gone more blonde (a dye job?), and even with her bruised face, I could remember the perfect teeth and the way she'd laughed so easily.

The front of her blouse had been ripped open to expose large breasts without a bra. Someone had probably used a knife to slit the front of her designer jeans and pulled them down around her ankles. They must have also used the knife on her—underneath her the grass was flooded with blood. In spite of all my training, I struggled to comprehend the horror of what I saw beneath me: the destruction of such a beautiful human being.

"M.E. been called?" Sonneson asked.

Before the young cop could answer, a van pulled alongside the fence, crumpling the dead leaves. It was brown, and lettering on the side read Hennepin County Medical Examiner. A woman flipped her legs out the door and jumped onto the ground. Dr. Helen Sohm. She carried a small black briefcase like doctors used to carry for house calls years ago. She circled around us to follow in the footsteps we'd taken earlier.

She began to examine the body while Detective Sonneson and I canvassed the area. Near the back wall of the church we found an area of ground that appeared to be disturbed. The scene of a fight?

With my mag light I traced a line from there toward Mackenzie. I saw it immediately: two parallel sets of foot marks that had crushed many of the leaves and the grass.

"Find any weapons?" I asked the young cop.

"Nope. But I haven't looked beyond the perimeter yet." When I stared at him, he continued, "I'll do it right now." He walked away behind the bobbing shaft of light from his mag.

"Look at this," Detective Sonneson said. He pointed his light at the ground. Along the side of the dirty white wall, there appeared to be some blood spatters. "Okay, so he starts with her here, she manages to get away, runs or fights with him, until she finally gives it up over there."

"Do you think it was a rape also?"

Sonneson shrugged. "Yeah, but we'll have to wait for the doc to confirm. Shit, this doesn't look good. No weapons, no car, and this ground cover will be impossible to get footprints from. Maybe that's blood on the wall, and maybe it's the killer's. That would help."

A feeling of intense loneliness washed over me. When I'd accepted the promotion, I never thought the first homicide I'd investigate would come so close to me. But I had a sworn duty to see this through and solve it.

Mackenzie Monroe had been the homecoming queen at Minnetonka High School. Beautiful, popular, and destined for success, of course. She hadn't known that Luke Smith existed back then, even though we shared tenth grade biology class and I sat right behind her for a year. She ignored my type in favor of the louder jocks that swarmed around her.

Until one night during our senior year. The basketball team had beaten Edina, and the students flooded out of the arena. I left in my parents' Saturn toward home when I saw someone walking on Highway 62—a dangerous place for anyone to be at night. As I got closer, I recognized Mackenzie and crunched to a stop in the gravel on the shoulder. I got out and identified myself. She asked, "Who?" I explained.

After a fight with her boyfriend, who'd dumped her out of his car, and with no cell phone back then, she'd started walking. Mackenzie agreed to a ride and got in with me. The temperature warmed immediately, although I'm sure it came solely from me. I felt moisture under my arms as I looked at her.

"Hey, thanks," she said. "Did we ever have a class together?"

The conversation lagged. I had no idea what I should say to someone like her. Her dark hair was so big and luxurious, her legs thin, and even though she had someone else's letterman's jacket on, I could make out her full figure. My throat felt thick, and I felt embarrassed to even be in the car with her.

Twenty minutes later, I dropped her off. She left the scent of her musky perfume in the car. I drove around the corner and stopped the car to breathe. Mackenzie had been so magnetic that I was tempted to fall in love with her right then. Ridiculous, of course, because she'd probably already forgotten about me.

But there was one thing that I remembered beyond her charisma, and it might be a clue to the lifeless body on the grass now. As she prepared to get out of the car, Mackenzie had smiled a white acre of teeth and paused to look at me. I saw something wild behind her eyes. Something maybe even crazy. Then she said thanks and was gone.

It wasn't until the next morning I found the chain and heart-shaped locket on the front seat that she must have dropped. I thought of giving it back, but it was the one thing that tied me to her. In an odd way, I felt she owed it to me.

"Hey, you still with us?" Sonneson interrupted my memories.

"Sorry. Yeah, of course." I shifted from one leg to the other. "What else should we do here?"

"Can't do much more tonight. Tape off the area and post a guard. We'll come back in the daylight."

We shuffled back to Mackenzie's body. Dr. Sohm, a tall woman with broad shoulders, grunted and stood up. "Looks like she was stabbed multiple times. Do we have a psychopath here? Can't tell for sure about sexual assault yet, but I'll do the autopsy first thing tomorrow morning."

"I'll be there." I volunteered before Detective Sonneson could. I'd give him a break as a way of saying thanks for his training. He and I went back to our vehicle. Thank God he drove. I don't think I could've done it. In the darkness, I turned my head so he couldn't see me blinking my eyes.

Dr. Sohm wasn't able to start the autopsy until late the next morning. I'd waited at the M.E.'s office all morning. Too long, as it gave me time to think more about Mackenzie.

After the ride I'd given her, we never talked again in high school. I held the fleeting belief that she remembered me and appreciated what I'd done even though all evidence pointed against it. I paid attention to her social career as we both finished school. I prayed that graduation would come so that I'd get over her. In my mind, I alternated between the temptation of loving her blindly and the humiliation of her ignoring me. I couldn't stand it much longer.

Dr. Sohm entered the waiting room, where I sat under a skylight. I could sense clouds crossing the sky by the gray tint to the light in the room. "I'm prepared to begin," she said and led me through three doors into the examination room.

Several steel tables were lined up in a row. A black man lay on one near the far wall. Dr. Sohm directed me to a closer table. I took several more sips of stale coffee along with deep breaths. After all the tempting fantasies about making out with Mackenzie Monroe and seeing her naked body in my arms, I now looked at a pale, limp shell of a once gorgeous human. Lying on her back, Mackenzie's stomach sagged so low it showed the bottom edge of her rib cage. Her pubic hair looked like a piece of steel wool. Worse, I saw dozens of slits across her body that looked like pairs of small closed lips. Stab wounds. As she gloved herself, Dr. Sohm's large, reddened hands contrasted with Mackenzie's delicate skin. I felt claustrophobic and turned away.

"You okay, Luke?" Dr. Sohm asked.

"First one. Mind if I pull it together over there?"

She laughed. "Don't worry. Happens to everybody. You'll get over it."

I knew I wouldn't get over this one.

Two hours later, she came out to the waiting room with preliminary results. Her breath smelled like spearmint. Dr. Sohm looked up as Sonneson clopped across the floor to meet with us. "Just in time," she told him. We all sat around a low table.

"These are my conclusions based only on the preliminary testing and examination. The cause of death was cardiac arrest as a result of severe blood loss and a blood pressure crash. I observed twenty-seven wounds in various places on the torso, probably caused by a knife. There were also contusions and fractures around the head."

"Was she sexually assaulted?" asked Sonneson.

"Yes. There was evidence of abrasions on the inner thighs. But there was no evidence of semen. I suspect the perp wore a condom."

"Any places where other bodily fluids had been transferred so we could try for a DNA analysis?"

"No, unfortunately. Which leads me to my greatest concern. Something beyond my medical expertise, I confess."

"What's your worry?" Sonneson sat forward.

"The victim had a blood alcohol concentration of .17 percent —high. So, was this a date rape? But then, the level of violence is so high, that leads to a troubling probability."

My stomach turned over, and I couldn't remain seated. I walked in a circle around the chairs.

"So, Doc, what's the bottom line?" Sonneson asked.

"I caution you, this is not my official opinion. I think you're looking for a very clever psychopath. He knows how to avoid leaving incriminating evidence of both the sexual assault and the murder. That's one dangerous guy. Maybe he's a medical student, a lab tech with knowledge of crime scene investigation, or maybe even someone in law enforcement."

"I see what you mean." Sonneson blew out a lungful of air. "It's like he created the perfect crime scene—for a killer."

"Worse. I'm not an expert, but I took some psychiatric courses in med school. With these kind of guys, it's like he had a 'mind out of body' experience during the event."

Even Detective Sonneson couldn't sit still. He stood, thanked Dr. Sohm, and led me out into the gray day. Across the street, the

Vikings football stadium soared into the clouds, dwarfing both of us. I followed him to our vehicle.

I cleared my throat. "Uh, there's something I have to tell you. I knew the victim in high school."

His eyes searched over my face. "Maybe you should request reassignment."

"I know, but I'm sure I can be objective. In fact, it will give me extra motivation to find her killer."

He thought about it and said, "Okay, for now. I'm trusting you to keep some emotional distance." He put his hand on my shoulder. "I know you may be tempted to cut corners in order to get the perp, but you can't."

How did he know I was already thinking that way? That I might be willing to jeopardize my training and career to bring her killer to justice? I had other investigative clues to check out, so tentative I didn't tell Sonneson about them. "Sure. Let's get back to the crime scene."

We entered Prospect Park again. The houses were built in many different styles, so many it looked as if they were assignments for dozens of graduate architects: Tudor, Prairie style, California rambler, Cape Cod cottages, Spanish, and even a few that resembled Minnesota ice fishing shacks. Feeble gardens struggled to survive in the final days of fall. But one garden, sheltered in the corner of the house, boasted lush red gardenias.

When we parked outside the fence and walked behind the church, the sun burst out and reflected off the wall. It warmed the back of my shoulders. I could smell someone burning leaves illegally. A tech was kneeling by the wall, scraping samples of what we hoped was the blood of the killer that could be identified. He looked up and squinted in the bright light.

"Hey, guys. I'll get this to the sheriff's crime lab ASAP, but it'll still take a couple days for test results."

"Sure." Sonneson moved across the lawn to a white outline of the body on the ground.

I saw matted leaves and indentations in the sod where a struggle must've occurred. Both of us squatted and duck-walked across the grass, looking for any clues left by anyone. Whoever had done it was good, real good at covering their tracks. I found a few of Mackenzie's things: a tube of Too-Too Bamboo lipstick and one of her shoes. A Pappagallo flat. Where was her purse? She always seemed to carry a big, gaudy purse, I remembered.

It had been several years after our graduation from high school. I hadn't even thought about Mackenzie until I was in a bar with a softball team of old friends from school. She suddenly blew into the bar with a bright green purse and found our second baseman. Mackenzie was drunk or high and acting crazy. Loose. Her blouse had fallen open while she hung over our teammate. Of course, she was charming and still beautiful. But why was she chasing the second baseman? He was a loser and mean when he was drunk. Her actions were irrational.

When he went to the bathroom, I pulled her aside and advised her to leave. I even offered to drive her home. She ignored me. All the old feelings flooded back to me. I realized that I was still in love with her, but at the same time, Mackenzie frustrated me at how careless she was about her safety. The crazy eyes, I thought. There's something wrong with her. But how could I use that clue to solve her murder?

"Bag those pieces of evidence," Sonneson reminded me.

I pulled several baggies from my pocket and put the debris of Mackenzie's final moments in each of them. How sad that the last reminder of her life was a tube of lipstick.

"Let's start with her work, her friends. Then we'll scope out the family." Detective Sonneson's words wound down in volume as if he were tired.

"Sure."

The next morning at 8:17, we entered the spacious lobby of the Thor Advertising Agency in downtown Minneapolis. We had an appointment to talk with a close friend of Mackenzie's, Norah Ash.

She shuffled into the lobby and twitched her head to one side. We followed her to a small conference room. It was gaudy with colors and shapes, and in the corner, a female mannequin stood covered by a lavender cocktail dress. The plastic head was missing. Ash broke down the minute we closed the door.

"I can't believe she's gone. So full of life, so fun, smart." Ash looked up at us with red-rimmed eyes. "And the horrible way she —Do you have the sicko who did it?"

I didn't know what to say, so Detective Sonneson began, "I'm sorry to tell you, no. That's where you can be a big help. Do you know who Mackenzie was dating? Who her friends were?"

"Her friends—they were all great." Ash swallowed and paused for a moment. "The guys in her life, well, that was Mackenzie's weakness. She seemed to attract the worst. I never could figure it out 'cause she was so beautiful."

"Any particular creep you might suspect?"

"That's easy." She coughed. "A bastard named Corky Tedeschi. Was with her every night. We doubled once, and I even told Mac, 'Never again.' I tried to warn her."

That reminded me of my experience with Mackenzie. After she had left the bar with the second baseman, I worried about her. I knew it was creepy, but I followed them for forty minutes. They got to her apartment, and both of them argued at the front door. I could see her wagging her head to say "no." Then he grabbed Mackenzie with both hands cupped around her butt. I was about to get out of my car. Instead of resisting him, she gave in and melted into his arms. I was torn between jealousy and an odd feeling of protectiveness. I was tempted to interrupt and replace the loser with me. Would Mackenzie treat me with the same passion?

"Do you know where Tedeschi lives? Where he works?" I asked.

"He always bragged about running some research lab in Northeast Minneapolis."

We left a few minutes later. Detective Sonneson said the obvious. "We need to shake down this guy."

I felt a surge of energy. Maybe we had a lead on the perp. Back at headquarters, we ran an NCIC computer search on the guy and finally came up with a hit. As we'd suspected, he had a rap sheet that included a DUI, but more critical, two violent domestic assault convictions.

That afternoon, we drove to Tedeschi's work address. I thought back to Mackenzie and the nights I'd followed her. I should have done something, should have warned her about the dangerous men she picked up. And there was an occasional woman, too. Even those ended up in fights with Mackenzie. I still loved her, in a weird way, but I also hated her for how she treated me. Why was I so obsessed with her? Maybe it was because I also remembered the night in high school when I found her, and how she had smiled at me and how vulnerable she looked. She was a beautiful piece of crystal that was cracked in a way that only I could see.

Detective Sonneson and I arrived at MeduTec Labs at 2:56 in the afternoon. We stopped at the front desk, badged the receptionist, and asked if Corky Tedeschi worked there. She made several calls and finally looked up at us. "He hasn't been at work for two days," she told us.

She gave us his home address in a far north side suburb. We tried to roust him but didn't find him there. The next door neighbor said he'd been missing for a while. Although the trail looked cold, we were certain we were onto the killer.

At our office, Sonneson applied for a warrant to search the perp's house. It would take a couple hours for a judge's review. I left for the bathroom. I needed some privacy to think. I wanted to bolt and break into the place myself before Tedeschi could cover up any evidence and get away. I struggled to calm myself, to follow the law in order to make sure it would be a clean bust when we found the asshole. Coming out of the stall, I washed and walked through the lobby.

Had Mackenzie's wildness finally gotten her into trouble that even her charm and beauty couldn't extricate her from? I cared for Mackenzie, but her behavior also caused me to boil with anger. How interesting that hate and love can be two sides of the same coin. Now it was too late for me to help her anymore, and I felt guilty. Maybe I should have done more.

My phone text pinged. It was Detective Sonneson: *Get back here now!*

When I got to our office, Sonneson told me a call had come in from Minneapolis P.D. A rookie said he'd been back at the crime scene and had found something at the church, beyond the fence and out in the street. I sat next to Sonneson's desk as he called the officer again and put him on speaker phone.

"It's a running shoe," the officer told us.

"So what?"

"Well, Detective, it's got some sod jammed into the toe."

Sonneson shifted his position in the chair. "Can you tell if it's a male or female shoe?"

"No. But I've got it bagged, and I'm on my way to forensics with it as we speak."

"Good work, Officer." He hung up. "Well, for now, we wait. These are the toughest ones for me."

"What's that?" I asked.

"We have so little evidence. The public thinks we solve every murder. Truth is, about thirty percent of 'em go unsolved for lack of evidence. I'm worried this may be one of those."

My stomach groaned. I was determined not to let that happen to Mackenzie. "What about Tedeschi?"

Sonneson shrugged. "It's the only lead we've got, but Luke, unless he confesses or we find a witness that can put him there, we ain't got much."

I nodded in reluctant agreement. "I'm going to follow up with her family."

In my office, I checked through an old reverse directory, in print, that listed the homeowner's name and family members who lived there also. I found Mackenzie and discovered she had a son named Charlie. It listed a phone number; I called. His grandmother answered and told me I could come over after dinner to meet him.

Mackenzie lived in White Bear Lake. I drove out there on Highway 61. I turned into the town that resembled a New England village at 6:23 and easily found her house. When I knocked on the door, an elderly lady opened to welcome me inside. Charlie sat at the kitchen island, watching something on his laptop.

11

I gasped when I saw him. He looked so much like his mother. The same luxurious hair and body shape. He had his head down so close to his computer, I wondered how he could even see it. He glanced at me with wet eyes.

I was finally able to pry Charlie away from it. I'm sure he was hesitant to talk because of his grief. I spoke softly to him and told him I was a friend of his mother's from high school. "Did your mother have any boyfriends recently?" I asked.

"Which of the derps you looking for?"

"Why do you say that?"

"Most of them dissed her all the time. Especially the last one. Corky."

"Yeah, we know about him. What time did he pick her up the night she disappeared?"

"Didn't. Dude didn't come around that night."

"Huh?"

Charlie keyed on his computer in a blizzard of strokes. "Someone else picked her up. Mom left about seven, and I happened to be outside. She didn't see me, but I followed her. She got into a car, and I saw it was a woman driving. They seemed friendly."

"A woman? Can you tell me what she looked like?"

"Nope."

The next morning, I was in the office early. Detective Sonneson arrived, and I gushed everything I'd discovered from Charlie. "The woman picking up Mackenzie got me thinking in a different way. What if they went to a bar and some guy hooked up with Mackenzie? If we could find the woman, she may be able to lead us to the guy who raped and killed Mackenzie."

"Trouble is, you said Charlie can't make the ID. Where do we start?"

"Go back through her friends—"

"That gal at the ad agency. Maybe she knows where Monroe hung out."

I called Norah Ash.

"Well, I didn't hang with Mac all the time. When we did, she always wanted to go to the Chocolate Martini. It's kind of a meat market, but it was fun to flirt with the dudes there. I was always careful. I'd guess she started there," Ash told me.

I followed up with Detective Sonneson. "Can we get into Tedeschi's place yet?"

"Shit, no. Judge wants more info from me. Gotta go back to the courthouse this afternoon." He sighed. "How about we shake down that bar tonight?"

By eight o'clock we were in the Chocolate Martini. It was a rooftop restaurant/bar that overlooked bustling Hennepin Avenue. An entire wall of floor-to-ceiling speakers rattled my teeth and made interviewing the patrons tough. Rows of palm trees created what architects called "conversation spots," although conversation was impossible in this place. Women in white sheer dresses who were unusually tan seemed to walk around aimlessly and alone.

Sonneson and I carried three good photos of Mackenzie and did the tedious work of investigation—we talked to everyone we could find who was cooperative. We had interviewed at least ten people before the bartender recognized Mackenzie.

"My name's Irving. Yeah, she used to come here a lot." Irving had stepped off to the side out of the line of heavy rock music. "Nice babe. I'm sure I talked to her a few times. Can't remember much except she drew guys like flies. You know the type?"

I nodded.

Irving was thin and had long hair that made him look like a hippie from the '60s. "I can't recall the specific night you're talking about, though. Did she ever come in with a woman?" He tilted his head to the side. "Maybe. I always had the impression she was just looking for benefits. Nothing serious. Not many people come here looking to get married." He laughed.

We weren't getting anywhere with the investigation. I thanked Irving and asked him, "I don't mean to pry, but your name is Irving and you don't look like a bartender for a place like this."

He laughed again. "I'm getting my doctorate in Chinese medieval history. This pays a hell of a lot better than a teaching assistant, I'm sorry to say."

We left discouraged and frustrated. Statistics and a cop's own sense of the rhythms of a case all told us the longer a case went unsolved, the harder it became. Sonneson dropped me at my car parked at the cop shop. We promised to meet early after sleeping on things.

The next morning, as we were talking back and forth about what we knew, Sonneson interrupted me. "Wait a minute. Something's been bothering me. In all the years I've investigated these kinds of crimes, the perp always—I mean *always*—leaves something on the body."

I must've frowned to show I didn't understand.

"Think about the act of having sex, even a rape. You'd leave something: drips from your prick, your sweat, saliva, blood, something that could be found and tested. But Dr. Sohm told us there was nothing on the vic. Something's wrong."

"Yeah."

Sonneson wrapped his legs around each other in a tortuous manner. "Okay, Luke. Tell me I'm crazy. Listen to this. What if there never was a rape?"

"Huh?"

"Other than the abrasions on the inner thighs, there was no forensic evidence of a sexual assault, was there? Could the abrasions have been caused by Mackenzie fighting with the killer?"

"What about the bruising in the vaginal area?"

"I dunno. Could someone have used a blunt instrument to create the bruising?"

A hollow feeling crabbed up my back. The hair on my arms tightened. "We should talk with Dr. Sohm again. See how she reacts to this idea."

We called for an appointment, drove the few blocks to the medical examiner's office, and found Dr. Sohm in the small lunch area next to the examination rooms. I couldn't imagine eating lunch that close to the work they did, but that's why they were doctors and I was a cop.

"Hello, guys." She looked up from her salad and smiled. A piece of lettuce was wedged between her teeth. "How may I help you?"

We sat on either side of her, and Detective Sonneson explained our theory. He asked about the bruising.

Sohm leaned back in the tan plastic chair. She wore a sleeveless blouse, and I could see the pumped muscles bunch along her arms. Cannons. "Good question. It's possible if the victim had wrapped her legs around the assailant to fight back, that action would leave abrasions."

"And what about the fact you didn't find any other bodily fluids on the body?" Sonneson pressed her some more.

Her eyes narrowed and she stared at him. "I don't know where you're going."

"I'm not going anywhere except to explore the idea the vic may not have been raped."

"That's contrary to my findings. After all, there was bruising in the vaginal area."

"But can you tell *what* caused that?"

Dr. Sohm blinked a few times. "Well, no, I can't say with medical certainty it was caused by a stiff penis, if that's what you're implying." She crossed her legs, and I noticed she had large feet, almost as big as a man's foot.

Sonneson didn't ask any more questions.

"So, you think you've solved it, huh?" She smiled in an odd way.

Something about that made me feel creepy. Uneasy. I told her about Charlie and the woman who had picked up Mackenzie. "I'm beginning to wonder if it was the woman who killed her, after all."

"But you're up against a wall, aren't you? Unfortunately, you can't really prove anything at this point." Dr. Sohm's head tilted back as she looked down her face at us.

"Not at this point," I admitted.

"That's what I thought." She shifted in her chair, looking comfortable. "You're going to make a good detective," she told me.

"Why do you say that?"

Another smile crept across her face, and she leaned toward me. "Well, you're here to see me, aren't you? I know you were close to Mackenzie. You loved her and had since high school, and you even followed her at times."

15

How did she know about that?

Dr. Sohm continued, "Oh, don't worry. I don't think you did it."

I felt sweat break out under my arms. I forced myself to look at her. Her eyes locked onto mine, and I almost choked. I saw the same wildness, the same hint of craziness in her eyes that I'd seen in Mackenzie's eyes. Then it disappeared. She laughed in a carefree manner, and I knew for sure.

I knew she was the woman who had picked up Mackenzie, she was the one who had taken her to Prospect Park, and she was the one who had killed her. She had faked the sexual assault somehow. But there wasn't any possible way we could prove it.

The Confession

She was too young to be a murderer. Fifteen. Of course, criminal lawyer Ted Rohrbacher had seen a lot in his career, but this one bothered him. He looked at Sally, sitting next to her parents on the leather couch in his conference room. She was thin, with blond hair plastered over her head like she'd just gotten out of a shower. Her feet, in red running shoes, swung back and forth across the carpeting. Nervous. When Sally looked up at Ted, he could see blue veins through the skin below each eye.

Ted had read the petition accusing her of bashing in the head of her pastor, Todd McWhorter, with a shovel. It had happened two months earlier at the Ministry of New Life site. It was a year-round church community in northern Minnesota. Sally's pale arms stretched out from a t-shirt that read *Jesus Is Cool* on the front. Could this kid have swung a shovel to kill a man?

In the silence of the conference room, a clock ticked—while Ted struggled with his desire to help her get out of trouble.

Sally's father, Cy Graco, pulled himself forward from the deep grasp of the couch. He raised his hand to make a point. Dirt stained the wrinkles around his knuckles. He cleared his throat. "We came to you, finally, Mr. Rohrbacher. We tried several other lawyers, but they wouldn't take the case. But this is our daughter we're talkin' about. Know what I mean?"

Ted did know since he had a child of his own. A jolt shot through his chest at the thought of Matt being charged with murder.

Mrs. Graco looked up with red-rimmed eyes. "We're at the end of our rope, and—"

Her husband cut her off. "So we came to you. Everybody says you take the tough cases. And you're good." His eyebrows moved up and down like two struggling caterpillars.

"Tell me what happened." Ted turned back to Sally.

17

She almost disappeared in the contours of the couch. "I can't remember everything—"

Cy cupped both palms in the air like he was shaking a bag full of flour, trying to get the truth out. "We sent her up there with Pastor McWhorter. Lots of us did."

"We trusted him," Mrs. Graco added.

"See, the church built a retreat for families up in Black Wing County. Pastor moved up there and asked us to send some of the most promising girls to live there. If you're a God-fearing man, you'll understand. We wanted our kids raised the right way. Know what I mean?"

"How long did Sally live there?" Ted asked.

"Ten months," Cy said.

"With other girls?"

"Yes, sir. And boys, too," he added quickly.

"Any other parents live up there?" Ted asked.

Cy glanced at his wife. Her eyes dropped along with her head. Cy answered, "No, but there were other adults, if that's what you mean. See, thing is, we knew Pastor was called to shepherd our flock of kids. Get 'em out of the garbage pit that's the public schools right now."

Ted nodded. He thought back to the facts alleged in the petition in juvenile court charging Sally with murder. A motion for certification had been filed by the prosecutor, who had easily won. The case had been moved to adult court. If Sally lost the trial, even at fifteen, she could possibly spend the rest of her life in prison—without any chance for parole.

In spite of Cy Graco's ramblings, he was right about one thing: the case was impossible to win.

Ted read the police reports in his hand. The facts looked horrible. Sally was accused of spending time around the pastor's cabin, which the prosecutor alleged to be part of the preparations for the murder. Two days before his death, Pastor McWhorter had publicly reprimanded Sally before the entire group, accusing her of not being faithful to Jesus or obedient to the pastor. Witnesses said she turned red with anger and stormed out of the meeting. That provided a motive when, during the night, she stalked the pastor as he left his cabin, waited while he smoked a cigarette, and struck him in the back of the head with a shovel. After he was down, she continued to strike him until he was dead.

The next morning, his body was discovered and the police were called. They did an investigation, questioning the girls and other people in the camp. Sally wouldn't talk at first, but she'd finally taken the police to the scene and shown how she'd staged the killing step by step. She'd confessed to everything.

A search of her cabin turned up a pair of jeans and a sweatshirt with brown stains, suspected to be McWhorter's blood. The clothing had been sent to the Bureau of Criminal Apprehension lab in St. Paul for DNA analysis. The testing was not completed yet.

Ted sighed and ran his hand through the thinning brown hair on his head. A year earlier, he'd taken on another impossible murder case. The pressure and fallout from that case had almost cost Ted his marriage.

He looked at Sally. She'd shifted away from her mother's side to create some space. Sally's fingers twisted around one another and revealed fingernails bitten short, some cracked down the middle.

The obvious analysis, Ted thought, was the simple one: a teenage girl gets mad, temper out of control, waits for the pastor, and in a rage of young fury, acts impulsively to kill him. From years of experience, he thought through the possible legal defenses. Could a case be made for manslaughter? Killing "in the heat of passion"? The penalty was a fraction of the time for premeditated murder. But the fact that Sally had stayed after the first blow and continued to strike the pastor's head showed premeditation—first degree murder.

Ted cleared his throat and said, "I'm sorry, but I don't think I'm the right lawyer for this case." He spoke in a soft tone, practiced and convincing. He didn't want a drawn-out scene. Get them on their way.

Mrs. Graco sucked in air with a gasp. Her shoulders quivered.

"Why not?" Cy Graco asked. "We really need help."

Those words tugged at Ted. He was a good lawyer. But this was a dead-bang loser of a case. It'd be endless nights of work, stress, and, in the end, a guilty verdict. He was too tired to take on the defense.

Then he looked at the young girl sitting on his couch. If his own son, Matt, were guilty of murder, wouldn't Ted still want the best defense mounted for him? Ted stood up from his chair and propped his hands on his waist, feeling the extra weight that had accumulated there. He dropped his hands. "I, uh, would like to talk to Sally in private."

"We're her parents," Cy protested. "She's just a kid, and besides, we're payin'."

"I know, but *she* would be my client, not either of you."

The caterpillars above Cy's eyes flattened in frustration but also acceptance. "Okay."

Ted offered the parents each a bottle of Dasani water and ushered Sally from the conference room into a smaller one across the hall. He offered her a leather chair. "Want some pop?"

"I don't drink pop." Her voice was flat, without life.

Ted took his time sitting down. He wondered how he could bridge the wide chasm between himself and this young girl in order to get the truth from her. "I have a son a little older than you," he offered. "Goes to college here in Minneapolis. Are you interested in college?"

"I was. But now . . . I don't know."

He tilted his head as if to get a better look at her. She was so thin, maybe her only hope in prison would be to slip between the steel bars and escape. He felt sorry for her. Maybe he should take the case. At least make sure she got a fair trial and all that justice required for her. "If I take your defense, Sally, anything we talk about is confidential. That means I can't repeat anything you say to anyone, not even your parents. I promise that."

She glanced up at him and dropped her eyes to the floor.

"I guess the main question I have is: why? Why did you do this?"

"Can I have some water?" Sally asked. Ted reached back to the credenza and grabbed a bottle. He unscrewed it and set it before her. When she lifted it to drink deeply, it left a partial ring of dampness on the table.

"I was mad at the pastor."

"I can understand that."

"I'm not sure *you* could." Her eyes blazed at Ted for an instant.

"Maybe not." He waited in silence.

Finally, she spoke again. "It's like I got so mad I couldn't stop myself."

Ted's trained mind swirled around more defense possibilities: a mental illness defense? After all, there were no other witnesses. Then he caught himself, remembered the evidence against her, and realized how hopeless it looked. What more did the prosecutor need for a sure conviction—a video documentary detailing every blow of the shovel with Anderson Cooper narrating? *Now let's replay that last shot from a different angle. You can see the curve of the shovel strike the victim's head just to the left of the ear—*

Sally swallowed some water and started talking again. "I had some friends up there. Other girls who lived there. We like, worked all day to clean and cook and take care of the camp. At night, we had long meetings with prayer and Pastor Todd preaching sermons on how we should be faithful to Jesus."

Ted's mind drifted.

"He always said that since our parents had put us in the camp, we should obey Pastor Todd. That he was like, a minister of the gospel, and he was the representative of Jesus on earth."

A tingling feeling crept up Ted's back. Creepy stuff.

"Sometimes, he got real excited and told us he was Jesus."

"What?"

"Well, not the real Jesus, but a form of him on earth."

Ted wondered if the parents of all the girls knew what Sally was telling him. He tried to interrupt Sally to end the interview, but her words tumbled out like a river crashing over rocks.

"Yes, and then he told us, like, we all needed to be saved. That meant we needed to read our Bibles all the time, pray, and obey him. He would question each of us alone with him. What were we doing for our salvation?"

"And did you—?"

21

Her face flushed crimson, and Sally talked faster. "I tried as hard as I could. But sometimes, the Bible stuff was like, boring. He'd get mad at us. Then we had to go to his cabin to explain, and it was really scary."

"Oh?" The pastor sounded like a control freak.

"He had this thick beard that always had crumbs stuck in it and was dirty. He'd stare at us for a long time before saying anything. I thought I would wet my pants, I was so scared."

"And there was the night when he yelled at you in front of everyone, right?" Ted said.

Sally blinked a few times. "Yeah. Like, that was the worst."

"So, you decided to finally take care of him by using the shovel." Ted paused and moved forward carefully. He didn't want to put words into her head, but maybe she had acted without thinking—something closer to manslaughter rather than premeditated murder. "Did you think about killing him?"

"I know it's a sin, but yes." Her mouth tightened. "I wanted him dead."

Ted sighed. Hopeless. He was about to stand up and usher her back to her parents with a quick comment about how sorry he was not to take the case and good-bye.

"I wanted him dead because he'd been raping me."

Even after weeks of investigation and legal research, Ted couldn't figure out a defense. He'd hired a child psychologist to interview Sally. Maybe there was some post-traumatic mental illness defense that Ted could use. After all, the pastor was a pedophile, and perhaps Sally had acted in self-defense. But that didn't work either. In order to prevail with self-defense before a jury, Ted would have to show Sally had felt an immediate, life-threatening act from McWhorter. If she had killed him during a sexual assault, that would be self-defense. But she had waited until later.

The prosecutor, Jane Quigley, was sympathetic but had a job to do. "Sorry, no deals on this one, Ted. I'll go easy on her during the sentencing."

Without a chance to plea-bargain a settlement of the case, Ted and Sally were forced to start the jury trial. She was presumed innocent unless proven guilty. Ted calculated that it might be remotely possible that one juror wouldn't be convinced of her guilt beyond a reasonable doubt and cause a hung jury—putting pressure on the prosecution to cut a deal for a plea of guilty and reduced sentencing because of the sexual assaults. It was the only shot Sally had.

He explained all of this to Sally and her parents.

"I appreciate what you're tellin' us, but we believe in miracles," Cy Graco insisted.

His wife nodded. "We trust you."

"Thanks, but it isn't about trust. It's about the evidence. It's all stacked against Sally."

He turned to look at her.

Her eyes had a vacant look, and she nodded her head as if she were listening to music through some ear buds. "Jesus will provide for me," she whispered.

The following morning, they appeared in the courtroom on the second floor of the old courthouse in Black Wing County. The oak counsel table had dark stains and a thin crack down the middle. Beneath it a wooden drawer could be withdrawn with a scraping sound. In the corner, a thirty-seven-star flag hung from the wall—the "Nebraska flag," the one in use when the courthouse had opened in 1870.

While waiting for the jury to be seated, Ted reviewed the list of witnesses the prosecution intended to call. He flattened the paper on the counsel table and showed it to Sally, who sat next to him. He told her, "The prosecutor has to notify us of any possible witnesses they may call. Quigley doesn't have to call every one of these people." Ted ran his finger down the list while Sally read silently along with him.

Dr. James Arnold, Assistant Medical Examiner, Marquette County
Rev. Tim Walters, Director, Ministry of New Life Camp
Dennis Chow, EMT with Regional Hospital

Sgt. Teresa Billey, Deputy Sheriff, Black Wing County
Emily Johnson, Two Harbors, MN
Reggie Snow, Dilbert, MN
Doris Claypatch, Brainerd, MN
Ava Grissom, St. Paul, MN

During the trial prep, Sally had identified the last four people as girls who had been at the camp with her and had become close friends. Ted had tried to interview them, but they all refused to talk with his investigator. Probably scared, Ted thought, or their parents didn't want the girls involved if possible.

Ted leaned back in his chair. This would be rough. Witness after witness would testify against Sally, with Deputy Billey ending the case by introducing Sally's confession of murder.

He glanced at Sally. Her head hung forward as she scribbled with a pen across a yellow legal pad. Big circles with happy faces drawn inside the lines. A defense lawyer must never become emotionally involved with a client. Ted couldn't help it. That was why he'd taken the case, and now he regretted the decision.

But someone had to help Sally, if only to hold her hand as the evidence crashed down around her.

The medical examiner, Dr. Arnold, stepped to the witness stand first. He told the jury about his expert qualifications and education —seven years performing autopsies for the county.

The prosecutor moved into the procedure used on McWhorter. "Can you tell us what you did to the victim?"

"I made an incision across the forehead, midway up from the eyebrows. Next, I rolled the epidermis backward over the crown of the head to expose the skull."

"What did you find?"

"I found the bone structure crushed in several places. The skull was almost entirely disintegrated around the crown."

"Would that include the facial area?"

"Yes."

"Can you tell us what may have caused the trauma?"

"Something blunt and hard. Something flat, as there were no deep lacerations such as a hatchet or a metal pipe would make."

"Would the damages be consistent with blows from a flat shovel?"

"Yes."

"And can you tell us what the cause of death was?"

"Yes. Multiple fractures and crushing of the skull from a blunt instrument that caused severe blood loss and trauma to the brain tissue."

"This wasn't an accident, right?"

"Oh, no. I was frankly surprised that there were so many blows to the head. Unusual, in my experience."

Quigley called the first responder, Dennis Chow, next. "What did you find upon arriving at the crime scene?" she asked.

"I saw a body, prone, face down near a lake. The ground was soft 'cause it'd just rained. Blood had splattered across the leaves and ground around the victim's head. Lots of blood. I found a shovel with what appeared to be blood on the handle and metal part."

"Was there anyone present with the body?"

"No. Well, the deputy sheriff directed me to the body and came with me. One of the other residents, a young girl, had discovered the body."

"Anything else?"

"Yeah. Like I said, the ground was soft, so I saw what appeared to be lots of footprints. All mixed up, like people had been dancing or jumping around."

"Objection," Ted shouted. "The witness is speculating on what may have happened, and it's prejudicial."

"Sustained." The judge agreed.

Quigley asked, "Were you able to identify any of the footprints?"

"Naw, too muddy."

When Sgt. Teresa Billey walked to the witness stand, the oak floor creaked in places. She answered the prosecutor's question: "I seized the alleged murder weapon, the shovel, bagged it, and delivered it to the Bureau of Criminal Apprehension lab in St. Paul on account of the fact we don't have one in our county."

"What did they find?"

"It was tested for blood type and fingerprints or DNA. The lab results identified the blood of the victim on the shovel, but no fingerprints were able to be developed. And no DNA was found to be tested."

"Did you seize any other evidence?"

"Yes. I found the defendant's clothing in her room." The deputy held up a rumpled set of clothing inside a plastic bag for the jury to see. "It had what appeared to be bloodstains on both the shirt and jeans. The BCA lab tested and found the victim's blood on Sally's clothing."

"Did you later have a conversation with the defendant, Sally Graco?"

"Yes. I advised her of her Miranda rights and called her parents. Sally waived her rights and agreed to talk with me."

"What did she say?"

"At first, she was quiet, cried a lot. She asked that her parents be present. Normally, we interview suspects by themselves, but I felt sorry for her, so I agreed. Sally told me how she'd been living at the camp for some months and how things had become much worse for her there."

"What did she mean by 'worse'?"

"The pressure from the victim to live up to a Christian standard. Sally tried but felt she was still a failure. I asked her if she had hit the victim."

"What did she say?"

"Sally admitted that she plotted how to kill Mr. McWhorter."

"She thought about it?"

"Yes. She planned it for several days. Sally knew he always went down to the lake just before bed to smoke a cigarette. Sally decided to take a shovel from the storehouse and hit him in the head."

"She told you this?"

"Yes. She snuck up behind him and hit him in the back of the head as hard as she could. He fell forward, and she walked up to his head and continued to strike the head with the shovel."

"How many times?"

"She didn't remember."

"Was anyone else present?"

"She didn't say."

The judge called for the noon recess and ordered everyone back at two o'clock to finish the remaining witnesses.

Ted had trouble standing. He was stiff and felt numb after listening to the damning evidence. He felt like taking Sally's hand, but of course he would never do that. He held the courtroom door open and turned her over to her parents.

Cy Graco's eyes moistened while he hugged his daughter. "Have faith. Remember, you are a child of God." He led her down the hall to lunch, his arm looped around her shoulders.

Ted wasn't hungry. He knew the jury would be sympathetic to Sally for killing McWhorter after what he'd done to her, but it still wasn't a legal defense. They'd have to follow the law and convict her. Ted's best work would happen at the sentencing, when the judge could take McWhorter's actions into account.

After lunch, Ted led Sally to the counsel table. He could smell the lemon odor of wood polish. He looked at her and saw her eyes were red. He touched her shoulder. "You okay?" he whispered.

She nodded.

"It'll be over soon. I'll try to make it as quick as possible."

"Kind of like the dentist drilling in your tooth?"

He grinned at her sense of humor under the circumstances. "Yeah, something like that."

Sally straightened in the chair and looked up. "I'll be okay," she said.

The prosecutor called the first girl who had lived at the camp with Sally, Emily Johnson. "Did you know Sally Graco?"

"Yeah, like she was my roommate at the camp."

"So, you were friends?"

"Yeah, like super close."

"Were you at the camp the night the victim was killed?"

"We all were. Reggie, Ava—"

"I'll come back to that. Was Sally with you that night?"

"Earlier, yeah. We had vespers in the big hall. It lasted longer than usual; then we were released to go to our rooms."

"Did you see where Pastor McWhorter went?"

"Down toward the lake."

"What else happened?"

"Uh—"

"I know this is hard, Emily. Tell us what happened. Did you see Sally down by the lake?"

"Yeah."

"What happened?"

"Well, she had a shovel with her and was standing kind of behind the pastor."

"And what did she do?"

"Nothing."

"Nothing?" Quigley lifted her head from the notes she'd been reading.

"No, nothing. I came up to her, and I knew what she was thinking. We all wanted to do it."

Quigley's voice cracked. "What, what do you mean?"

"We, uh, wanted to, uh, kill him."

"You wanted to kill him?"

"Like yeah. He was so mean to us, and after what he'd done to Sally . . ."

"What was that?"

"Don't want to say. But I decided since she was my best friend and we'd both been saved by the blood of Jesus the month before, I would help her."

"What happened?" Quigley's voice sounded hollow.

"I killed him. I took the shovel from Sally and hit him in the head. Lots of times. Can't remember how many, but he fell and I kept hitting him. I hated him."

Quigley's face glistened with sweat. She fumbled with her notes. "Uh, that's all. No more questions for this witness."

Ted looked at Sally. She remained expressionless. He leaned over to her and said, "What's going on? I never saw this in any of Emily's recorded statements."

Sally shrugged and continued to look forward.

Carefully, Ted cross-examined Emily—mostly to get her to repeat her story for the jury again.

Quigley called the next girl, Ava Grissom. The prosecutor took her through her time at the camp and her friendship with Sally. "Did you see anything happen at the lake between the pastor and Sally?"

Ava paused and then said, "Well, she was standin' there with the shovel."

"Did she strike the pastor?"

"No. I did. 'Cause she was my best friend, and on account of what he did to her."

Quigley flopped back in the chair. She waited a minute and leaned forward. "So, you're saying you killed Pastor McWhorter?"

"Yes. I hit him with the shovel."

"Was this after Emily hit him?"

Ava frowned. "Who said Emily was there? It was only me and Sal. I saw what she was gonna do, so I did it for her. Afterward, I prayed to Jesus for forgiveness, and I received it from Him 'cause He loves me."

Quigley called Reggie Snow next. "Did you see Sally hit the pastor with the shovel?"

Reggie's face pinched around her mouth. Her eyes floated up to the ceiling. "No. I didn't see Sally hit the pastor 'cause I hit the pastor."

"I suppose Emily and Ava weren't there?"

"No, they weren't. I yanked the shovel from Sal and hit the piece of shit." She jerked in the witness chair. "Oh, I'm sorry. I mean I hit the pastor in the head. Lots of times. I heard his head crack, and I kept hitting. Blood shot up like a water fountain."

Reggie left the witness stand. Quigley stood to tell the judge the state was done with testimony, had no other evidence to present, and chose not to call any other witnesses. The government rested.

Ted thought quickly. The defense had the opportunity to present evidence, although he had not developed any during the investigation. He could call Sally, but Ted was worried she would repeat her confession—this time while under oath. Instead, her Fifth Amendment rights allowed her to remain silent and not say anything. The jury had already been instructed on this basic principle.

Ted had a better idea. Under Rule 26.03, Subd. 18 of the Minnesota Rules of Criminal Procedure, he could try an unusual tactic —ask for a judgement of acquittal. The rule allowed the defense to ask the judge to find the defendant not guilty even before the jury decided. If the judge thought the government's evidence was weak enough, the motion could be granted.

Ted stood and made his motion for judgement of acquittal.

The judge nodded and said he needed time to review the case. Two hours later, he returned to the bench and the courtroom came to order. "After reviewing the motions filed, pleadings filed, the forensic evidence, and all the testimony presented in this trial, I will grant the defense motion and find the defendant not guilty of first degree murder."

Revenge

Sheriff Todd Simmons vowed to get John Hammersmith before the end of his term in office. Simmons had just returned from a strategy session with the local prosecutor, who had told Simmons that unfortunately, he couldn't prove Hammersmith guilty—although they both knew he was guilty of murder.

A month earlier Hammersmith, one of the biggest shake-down men in Sakatah County, had killed Dale Vinkemeier. Dale had worked as an enforcer for Big John to coerce small businesses to pay for "insurance" against fires and damage. Big John had killed him in spectacular fashion. As a warning to other people who tried to cross him, Hammersmith had given Dale an overdose of heroin, to which Dale was addicted, and propped him in the passenger seat of Dale's 1997 Plymouth convertible. Then Big John drove the convertible to Dale's home at night and left him in the driveway for his family to find later. Hammersmith had even left a cold six-pack next to the body as a present.

Sheriff Simmons had grown up in the county, graduated from high school, and won first place in the state wrestling tournament in the heavyweight division. Although he left for two years of mechanic's school, he'd returned to his hometown. He had a talent for fixing machines, but Todd wanted to do something more important for his hometown. He'd run for sheriff against an incumbent who'd let the county go to hell. Todd had won. Still, the mechanic remained in him, and he always carried a tool box with him for puttering. But now, with only four months left in his term before the next election, Todd was determined to clean up the criminal element that had grown in the county since he'd left. It was going to be difficult.

He'd made a good start in the past years, but it hadn't been enough. The crime stats showed an increase that upset the city council and could affect Todd's reelection chances. Now he'd have to take drastic action.

It wasn't just the serious thugs like Hammersmith that Simmons wanted to eradicate; it was also the bothersome crooks that preyed on the local people. Vangie Connors, for instance. A cheap tramp in Todd's opinion, she was a bleached-blond, busty woman who wore tight t-shirts and had a tattoo down her leg that read "Lowell" in remembrance of her boyfriend, who now lived in Stillwater prison. Vangie was a "booster" from the old school. The manager of the Supply Depot big box store had told Simmons, "She has a specially designed coat, lined with dozens of pockets and augmented with straps to hold heavier merchandise. When she enters the store, she grabs whatever fits into the pockets of the coat. Our biggest losses are the power tools."

"She probably fences those all over the county," Todd said. "Do you have video of her boosting things? Any proof I could use in court?"

The manager shook his head. "Nope. She's too good. She always seems to know enough to drop the items just before I've stopped her in the store. I can't catch her."

When Todd got back to his office, his part-time secretary said, "Don't forget about the fundraiser. Sheri Booth called this morning. She's mad as hell."

Todd felt tightness across his back. "Yeah. I'll call her." Booth, president of the Junior Chamber of Commerce, had called about the upcoming Sakatah County fair. It was the largest fair in southern Minnesota and featured free corn on the cob, served hot in long metal trays. The fair had grown to include dozens of other food vendors, live musical entertainment, farm implement displays, and a huge midway with the most up-to-date rides. The Chamber depended on revenue from the fair for a big portion of their yearly budget. Todd had volunteered to be the chairman of the fundraiser this year.

He knew it would be helpful for his re-election chances if he was able to beat the dollar goal set last year. But how to do that? Todd wondered.

Of course, he had already talked with every business person in town, met with the volunteer groups like the firefighters and Scouts, and coordinated with every lawyer, banker, and accountant in the county. When Todd added up the pledge numbers, they fell far short of the goal reached the previous year. He had to find a new group of people who would contribute for the cause.

Sheri Booth's voice was insistent when Todd returned her call. "Sheriff, you know how important this is to all of us." Her words trailed off as a warning. "And we don't have much time left. You support us and we'll support you."

"I'm working on it," he assured her.

When he hung up, the tightness in his back spread to his chest. Holding the office of sheriff of Sakatah County was the best job he'd ever had—and he meant to keep it.

Another call came into the office. The cop from Union Hill, a small town on the western edge of the county, was calling. "Sher'f, you'd best get out here. It's a damn cryin' shame what's happened, but it's outta my jurisdiction."

"What happened?"

"Child abuse—sort of. It's too hard to explain. Can you make it out here?"

"On my way," Todd said. He tightened the brown necktie around his throat, wrapped the belt with his service weapon, cuffs, and speed loaders around his waist, and left for the official car. It was late July, and the little county seat where Todd worked dozed in the afternoon heat. Grasshoppers popped out from the dried grass in the parking lot, and when he got into the car, the heat took his breath away. The steering wheel hurt his fingers.

He turned onto County Road 23, which aimed straight west until it ran into South Dakota. Along both sides of the road, green corn stretched out in straight rows to the north and south. A breeze lifted the tassels on the plants to make them look like they were growing wispy yellow hair.

Simmons drove past the fairgrounds. At the entrance, an old wooden arch still stood after sixty-seven years. The paint—yellow and green to remind people of the corn theme—probably hadn't been touched up since before his birth. He slowed to glance into the grounds. Dozens of people worked inside. Some moved small kiosks that would hold greasy food when the fair opened in a week. On the far side were the steel bones of the permanent midway rides: Tilt-a-Whirl, the double Ferris wheel, bungee jumping, and the "Bone Shaker." It was the only one that Todd refused to ride. It used to be called a roller coaster, which had the connotation of some speed, but within reason. The Bone Shaker was designed to scare the crap out of the riders by rising high above the fair and then plummeting to earth as fast as a string of steel cars could fall. At the last second, with only a few feet left before crashing, the cars jerked to the left, corkscrewed 360 degrees, and shot up into the air again like a test pilot trying to break the sound barrier.

He remembered the problem in Union Hill, and Todd hurried back onto Highway 23. But he kept thinking about the Bone Shaker. Scary ride.

When he entered the crossroad of Union Hill, the local police officer was waiting at the stop sign.

"Hey, Murph," Simmons called to him. "Where do we go?"

"We can walk." The officer turned left down the one sidewalk in town. "Down at the end. Son of a bitch. I'd like to shoot the bastard," Murphy said quietly.

They reached a double-wide trailer home, set on blocks that used to be gray but were now black with age and inattention. "Name's Jones." He knocked on the aluminum door.

A rotund man opened the screen and frowned at the two law enforcement officers. "What the hell? Can't you keep your nose out of this?" he said. "I'm a business owner and I pay my taxes. I've been repairing small engines for years."

"Let's just talk," Todd offered. He smiled broadly, knowing it usually cooled off most offenders long enough to start talking. "Come in?" Todd said as he pushed his way through the door without a response from Jones.

In the small living room, Mrs. Jones dropped her head at the sight of the officers and scurried into a back bedroom. Murphy began, "Mr. Jones here was upset that his kids were screwing around, so he warned them to stop or he'd take away their pets. Gerbils. Well, as kids usually do, they kept it up, and he took it out on the animals." Murphy scowled at Jones.

"What happened?" Simmons asked.

"Jones went into the kids' rooms, took out their gerbils from the pens, and went to the back yard with all of them. One by one, he shot the little critters out of an air gun across the yard. If they didn't die that way, he drowned 'em in a pail of water right in front of the kids."

Jones stood up. He yelled, "I don't have to take this. Get out. I didn't commit any crime, and you know it."

Unfortunately, Jones was right. Maybe a cruelty to animals charge, but that was a misdemeanor, and Todd could already hear the prosecutor laughing at him—even though what Jones had done was despicable. They both left the trailer.

On his way back to the office, Sheriff Simmons received an emergency call. This time, it was a dead body at a home in town. He activated his siren and raced back along Highway 23. He called ahead to the county crime lab to meet him at the scene. When he got to the house, the medical examiner was already there with the local police.

An older woman sat in a bench on the front porch. She wore a hot pink halter top, shorts, and a straw snap-brim hat on the back of her head, a hat like Frank Sinatra might have worn. Sweat moistened her forehead, but she didn't look like she was mourning anything.

Todd walked up the steps and introduced himself.

"Candy Monson," she replied. "I own this dump." Her eyebrows bumped up and down. "Can't believe it. In my own house."

"What happened?"

"Uncle Carl lived upstairs for years. We all knew he was kinda diff'ernt. Hadn't worked on account of his disability. Stayed in his room a lot. We knew he was dealing meth, but what the hell? I didn't care so long as he and his low-life friends didn't cause no trouble. Couple days ago, this dude came over again. Dontell Green. He went up to Carl's room like usual to buy meth. We didn't think nothing

35

of it. He was up there a long time. One of my kids says she thought she heard a couple a pops. Then, dude comes down and boogies."

"Did you investigate upstairs?" Todd asked her.

She shook her head. "No. Why should we? Then, about three days later, we noticed Carl hadn't come down for anything, so we went up and found him dead. A bullet through the head." Candy took a deep breath. "Didn't smell too good."

"You sure it was Dontell Green?"

"Who else? Plus he's the only colored dude in the county. Hard to miss."

"Would you be able to testify about—"

Monson stood abruptly. "Naw. What? One a my kids heard a pop? What the hell would that prove?"

She was right. Without an eyewitness to the shooting or more evidence that Green was the killer, Todd couldn't prove much. Maybe the forensic people would find something. He sat next to her on the bench and felt more frustrated than ever. All these criminals were living openly in the county, and he couldn't get rid of them.

Two hours later, Simmons was back in his office. A small window air conditioner whined with the effort of cooling the space. His budget had been cut, so a new unit was out of the question. He'd printed several spreadsheets about the fundraiser, and they lay across his desk. The numbers looked awful. Plus, he'd already fielded two calls from the media about the death of Carl at the Monson house. Soon they'd print the story about Todd's failure to stop crime in Sakatah County. Two murders in less than two months.

Then the TV stations from the Twin Cities had contacted him, demanding on-camera interviews. That was the last straw, and Todd had hung up on them all. He had to act.

His mind drifted to the county fair. He'd been attending since he was a kid. It had been a long tradition to offer free corn on the cob. The fair even sponsored an eating contest to see who could gobble up the most corn. But unlike everyone else, Todd didn't like corn. Hated it, actually. He pictured the cobs with their rows of yellow kernels that were always crooked.

An idea struck him, and he leaned forward in the chair.

If he couldn't prove the cases against the criminals in the county, maybe Todd could at least shake them down for a contribution to the fundraiser. No—the idea was too crazy. He stood up. It wouldn't work.

But maybe it *would* work. They understood that Todd knew of their guilt. Maybe he could threaten them enough to cough up money for the fundraiser.

Of course, it must be done quietly. If the Chamber ever knew where some of the money had come from . . . Well, he'd be out of office so fast he wouldn't have time to turn off the air conditioner.

The idea grew in his mind as he devised ways to corner the scum of the county. He'd hint that prosecution was inevitable unless they made a contribution. In turn, Todd would offer them free tickets on the rides at the county fair. To an outside observer, it would look like a legal trade—contribution money for some rides. No one would ever suspect what Sheriff Simmons had really done to get the money.

The next morning, Todd strolled to the local diner, Neumann's Organic Restaurant—although nothing on the menu was remotely organic. He saw Vangie Connor at the counter in her usual place, where he had hoped to find her. He sat next to her, ordered the thin Norwegian coffee, and said to Vangie, "How's business?"

Even though it was a no-smoking diner, she smoked the last of her cigarette, blew a big lungful of air onto the eggs before her, and replied, "What's this about, Sheriff?" She had pale skin, with new pimples across her nose, and her hair was still wet from a morning bath.

"I'll get right to the point, Vange. You know I'm facing re-election this fall. I'm starting a crackdown on people like you. I've got a new budget that will fund help from the big boys in Minneapolis to come down with their experts," he lied to her. "I've vowed to get people like you off the streets for good."

Vangie's shoulders shook as she started to laugh. She stopped when she turned to look at Todd. His eyes bored into her, and she knew something was different this time. "So, what the hell do you want from me?"

Todd glanced behind them. Two people huddled in a booth on the far side of the diner. He leaned closer to Vangie. "See, I've got another problem. The fundraiser at the county fair needs contributors. Let's make a deal. When the law enforcement from Minneapolis gets here, I'll 'forget' to tell them about you. But I need a generous contribution from you in return."

She ran her hand through her hair and didn't respond for a long time. Finally, she sighed, "How much?"

In five minutes, Todd had his money and had given her free tickets for admission to the county fair and the rides. He left quickly. In the next two days, he managed to round up Big John, Jones the gerbil killer, and even Dontell Green, among dozens of other scumbags in the county. Each of them, after some persuasion, had contributed to the fundraiser. Todd gave them all free tickets and warned them to be at the fair on Friday night at eight o'clock—as he would be there watching for them. "To make this look legit, you gotta get on the rides," Sheriff Simmons ordered them all. "I'll be at the Bone Shaker."

By Friday morning, the spreadsheets on Todd's desk looked completely different. He'd not only made the numbers for the goal but had surpassed last year's figures. He took a long lunch and drove out to the fairgrounds by late afternoon.

The sun glowed through the arch, giving the illusion of gold laminate to the old wood. The transformation looked magical. He was allowed to drive the official squad car into the grounds. Before he got there, he could smell the food. Out of the car, Todd strolled up the dusty street to the corn on the cob booth. He was hungry. Shallow trays of butter held endless corn cobs, each of them golden as they rolled back and forth in the liquid. Todd selected a hot dog instead, took it from the server, and shook mustard over it in a long yellow squiggle.

As he started to eat, the attendant yelled, "Watch out!"

Todd jumped out of the way as one of the tables buckled from the weight of the corn and collapsed. The tray fell, butter slopped out of the end, and dozens of cobs bounced off the ground to roll away in dirty trails.

The attendant squatted over the cobs. "Well, we can write their obituaries."

Todd finished his hot dog and walked back to the squad car. He glanced behind him. Three people were watching. "Dog loose," he shouted and hurried to the Bone Shaker as if he were chasing a dog off a leash—a misdemeanor offense. He ducked underneath the ride and remained hidden in the shadows for a short time.

By eight o'clock, the fair was filling with people. Since there wasn't much else to do in the county, everyone attended the festivities. Todd looked for the "special donors." Had he threatened them enough to actually show up? He waited. Ten minutes later, he finally saw Vangie Connor approach the ride. She was followed by Big John and three heavy thugs with him. Soon, all of the sheriff's "people" were there. He stood near the entrance and made sure to allow only the criminals onto the ride. "A special party," he told other people as he turned them away. Soon, the thugs had filled the Bone Shaker.

The operator closed the protective railings in each car against all the riders and signaled the other man to start the ride. The engine chugged into low gear. Metal screeched against metal as the ride came to life. Slowly, the cars clanked up a steep incline. Some people started to scream in anticipation.

The sheriff watched as the cars crested the top high in the air, did a corkscrew, and came hurtling down toward the ground. The screaming sounds followed the falling cars like smoke trailing from a locomotive traveling at top speed. As the line of cars started into the 360-degree corkscrew at the bottom, there was a screech of bending steel. Then the rails separated and the cars flew off the ride. They launched into the air, free of any restrictions, while the screaming grew to a frightening new level. Then the cars crashed back to the dirty ground, smashing together in a tremendous explosion of metal and bodies squashing into each other.

When the dust settled, Sheriff Todd Simmons pushed his way through the stunned crowd of people looking at the wreckage. Even even though he knew all the dead bodies were the scumbags and murderers of the county, it was still his job to investigate the tragedy, and he meant to do his duty. Before he reached the victims, he looked under the ride to make certain he hadn't left any of the tools he'd used earlier.

Eat, Prey, and Maybe Die

Poison. If he was going to do it, poison might work best. Ethylene glycol was colorless, odorless, and slightly sweet to the taste. It would be fatal in under an hour and difficult to detect. A food chemist at Nature's Best Food Company, Bob Crane daydreamed about the mechanisms to deliver the poison. A fancy cocktail. Perfect. But an autopsy could be risky.

Maybe Bob could use a gun to the head. Easy, quick, fatal. But then he'd have to find an unregistered gun and learn to use it. And with all the technology available to crime scene detectives, he was sure they could trace a gun to him somehow.

Drowning? Car accident? He realized it was actually difficult to kill someone you hated and get away with it. He could go to her house and whack her in the head with a brick or heavy pan. Too messy. Too much evidence could be left behind.

His boss, Lois Cohen, had fired Bob's lover from her job in the lab where they both worked. "Doesn't fit our culture," Cohen had said. Crushed, Terri had left town—and Bob. He would never forgive Cohen for ruining his only chance at happiness.

Now, standing in his kitchen, Bob waited for the "boss from hell." In a few minutes some of his friends from work would also arrive. He'd scheduled the brunch prior to Cohen's firing of Terri. Reluctantly, he had decided to keep the date—if for nothing else, to try and stay on Cohen's good side himself.

Contentiously divorced, he was paying exorbitant child support payments for his daughter, Ava. Bob didn't begrudge the higher costs, but now his salary was stretched to the breaking point. He had been lonely for years, until he met Terri. Her memory hung on like a ghost.

He unscrewed a bottle of dried cilantro and sniffed. Not good enough, he decided. This meal must be special for his friends. Bob pulled out a bunch of cilantro from the refrigerator. It smelled grassy and sweet and left a spicy prickle in his nose.

Mexican food was everyone's favorite. Bob had chosen that for the main course: Bobby Flay's ranch-style eggs with chorizo and tomato-red chili sauce.

He set his bamboo cutting board on the counter and placed eight ounces of chorizo sausages on it. The recipe said to remove the skins, so Bob went to the drawer next to the sink. His fingers crawled over the handles of the Wusthof knives.

He cupped a sausage in his palm. It felt as soft as a baby's skin. He inserted the tip of the steel knife at the lower end of the meat and pricked the skin, sliding the blade underneath. What would it feel like to plunge the knife into living flesh?

Bob worked upward along the length of the sausage. When he got to the top end, he used his fingers to spread the skin and unwrap it carefully from the meat inside. He smelled the spicy aroma with hints of hot, dry deserts far to the south of his home in Minneapolis.

Cohen had been his boss for three years—three years of hell. In her fifties, she had put on weight but still wore short skirts that were as tight as the skins he'd just stripped off the sausages. The arrogant, ignorant "drill sergeant" oversaw Bob's research lab.

With her as his boss, Bob's workload had doubled. That made her team meetings even more maddening. The Bitch scheduled them and everyone was expected to attend. Bob flashed back to the meeting last week. She had made her entrance twelve minutes late while seven people waited. As she sat down, her phone hummed the Neil Diamond song "Cracklin' Rosie." It sounded like a social call. After eight minutes of moronic chatter, she hung up and dismissed everyone. Bob had lost over twenty minutes from his pending projects, and he knew there would be hell to pay.

He searched through his wine and selected a Montepulciano for the chili sauce.

Bob removed a saucepan from the lower cupboard. He set it on the stove and added canola oil to heat up. He arranged the sausage into the pan. With a wooden spoon, Bob crumbled the meat. It sizzled and released a pungent aroma of spices.

The doorbell rang. With long strides, Bob loped through the living room to the front door. He opened it to see Jo Ann, the chemist who worked in the lab next to his. She smiled, stood on her tiptoes, and pecked him on the cheek. "Hey, it's Emeril himself." She laughed. "Naw, you're too skinny." Her hair smelled like herbal shampoo.

Bob hurried back to the kitchen, followed by Jo Ann. "Thanks for coming early. I could use some help."

Jo Ann clinked a bottle of Jose Cuervo Blanco tequila onto the counter. Next to that she emptied a mesh bag of limes. They rolled around in crooked paths. "This okay for your margaritas?"

"Sure. I make 'em from scratch." Bob hovered over the spitting saucepan. He used a slotted wooden spoon to lift out the golden brown meat and set the clumps onto some paper towels. "I'll be sure to give Cohen a triple shot. That'll finish her off."

"You should substitute drain cleaner," Jo Ann whispered.

"Too messy. I'd have to clean up."

"Okay, I know I promised not to talk about her, but you know what she pulled yesterday?"

Bob snapped a can opener onto a can of Hunt's whole peeled plum tomatoes and twisted the handle as it crawled around the rim. "Nothing will surprise me."

"Okay, so she's always saying her nephew's got ADHD, right? Well, she ordered me to head up a charitable drive for an ADHD counseling center. Not even remotely work related! Wasting company resources! Ask me, I think the kid needs to get out of her clutches."

"He's a charity that's always been close to your heart," Bob kidded Jo Ann.

"Shut up. Okay, I know damn well once I've worked my ass off, Cohen will take the credit."

"She always does."

Jo Ann pounded her fist on the counter. "Take that, you freak!" she shouted. "Not that I'm defending her, but I'm impressed that she has taken such good care of her nephew. Too bad Cohen can't bring some of that charity into the office."

"Meanwhile, squeeze the limes for the margaritas. I'll prepare one for the She-wolf of the SS." He emptied the tomatoes into a small bowl and poured almost all the oil out of the pan. Next, he rolled a Spanish yellow onion onto the cutting board. He selected the chef's knife, twelve inches long and almost two inches deep.

Gripping it tightly, he cut down in the middle of the onion. The skin crackled, clear juice ran out, and the left side fell away. Bob blinked as the oils floated up into his eyes. Placing the tip of the knife on the board, he levered the blade up and down across the rings to chop them. He heard the crisp sound of the blade severing the pieces into square chunks. While his eyes stung, the sound of the knife chunked against the bamboo over and over.

Bob thought of Terri. It had been such a struggle for Bob to date again after the debilitating divorce, but Terri had coaxed him along. Bob's vacant and narrow life had blossomed for the first time. Now, without Terri, his future collapsed like a dead plant before winter. They had tried to maintain a long-distance relationship, but it hadn't worked.

"I got a better story," Bob said to Jo Ann. "Last summer she got tickets for a Twins baseball game. Said it would be a 'team building' event. But there was no requirement to attend, so I spent the day with Ava. Did I get shit from her! Told me it would definitely affect my future with the company." He poured tequila, lime juice, and triple sec into a steel shaker filled with ice. Bob shook it roughly and heard the ice clatter against the steel. He poured out two drinks into frosted glasses.

"That's bullshit." Jo Ann sipped her drink. "Oh, is this good."

"Glad you like it. Cooking and entertaining are about the only things that give me pleasure anymore."

Jo Ann's face wrinkled. "I bet Cohen will be late, as usual, so she can make a grand entrance."

"When she drives, the sun visor is always down so she can look in the mirror all the time." Bob used the knife to scrape the chopped onions into the pan. "All she talks about are her problems. Her job, her weight, her heart problems. It's only her malicious personality that keeps her going."

Bob unwrapped five cloves of garlic. Using the flat side of the chef's knife, he placed it on top of a clove and smacked the blade with his palm. Smashing a skull would feel good. Underneath, the garlic split open and the husk fell off, leaving the smashed cloves. In the pan with the onions, the garlic turned walnut brown as it released a pungent odor.

He glanced at his watch that hung loose on his wrist. "Dammit! I forgot to fix a dessert." He sighed. "I want this to be perfect so that you can't even detect my presence in the preparation."

Jo Ann said, "Don't worry. You've got all this fruit for dessert. Who else is coming?"

"Gary and Maureen."

"Gary?" Jo Ann's eyes opened wide. She slammed the margarita glass on the counter. "Are you really being mean? Do you know what our *beloved leader* did to him?"

"No, what?" He turned down the heat on the pan.

"She gave him a big research project. Told him he was completely in charge. But then she interfered every half hour for days until he finally snapped. I know this is a time when you guys are supposed to let your feminine side out, but for God's sake, the guy actually cried."

"That's horrible." On the cutting board, Bob lined up a bright red jalapeño pepper, an ancho chili, and a pasilla chili that was black and shriveled like a raisin on steroids. They looked harmless lying there. But the combined heat of these ingredients could be deadly hot. Bob stretched on a pair of latex gloves and used his paring knife to attack the jalapeno pepper first. Maybe he should add a ghost chili to sear the lungs, throat, and tongue. Wouldn't kill her, but it would cause great pain. Bob smiled.

The sharp blade hesitated at the resistance of the outer skin. Bob sawed back and forth and burst through into the soft flesh underneath. The pungent smell irritated his nose. He chopped the pepper over and over. The recipe called for a coarse cut, but he got carried away and mutilated the pieces until they were scattered over the board in tiny bits.

The front doorbell rang again.

Bob took a deep breath, stopped cutting, and went to open the door. Maureen reached up to give him a loose hug. Their faces didn't touch. "Sorry, I'm early," she said.

"No problem. Jo Ann's here, and I'm making margaritas." Bob stepped aside as she walked toward the kitchen. Maureen opened her offering: two bags of tortillas. "I could only find flour, no corn. Sorry it's not more authentic."

Bob stripped off the gloves and waved his hand to indicate that was all right. "I still have to make the chili sauce." He pulled out another saucepan and set it on the stove.

"Why are you being so nice to the Wicked Witch of the West?" Maureen asked him.

Jo Ann said, "He's sucking up for a promotion."

"Hope you have better luck than me. She told me that with my resume I wasn't promotable," Maureen said. "Don't tell anyone, but I'm out of the lab as soon as I can find anything else." She accepted a drink from Bob.

He nodded with understanding. "I'm really doing this for all of you. And considering how she dumped Terri, it doesn't hurt for me to stay on her good side."

Maureen shrugged. "I hope you're right."

Bob glanced away to avoid answering. Terri's ghost always hovered near Bob.

"Hey, someone's at the door." Maureen left the kitchen and came back with Gary. He was short, with red hair and a bushy beard. From a paper bag he lifted out a six-pack of Corona beer, slick with moisture. "Hey, man. Put these in the fridge." He high-fived Bob. "Dude, the only reason I'm here is 'cause of you. I sure as hell wouldn't come for HER."

"We could write a new TV series called *Horrible Bosses*." Jo Ann laughed.

From the top cupboard, Bob lowered a Cuisinart food processor onto the counter. He poured the plum tomatoes into the top of the processor and watched as the red globs splashed over the gleaming blades at the bottom. Dump her in a cement mixer.

Bob added one cup of the wine into the pan with the onions and chorizo. As the mixture thickened, he scraped the coating off the bottom of the pan. He felt the glaze breaking up, and he increased the pressure. The glaze cracked and broke into jagged pieces that Bob smashed with the flat end of the wooden spoon.

Maureen stirred her margarita with a fingertip. The citrus smell wafted through the kitchen. "Uh, anyone know about the rumors of some more layoffs?"

"Huh?" Bob felt a jolt shoot through his chest. The payments for his daughter were already bankrupting him. He couldn't afford to lose his job.

Gary took a long drink of Corona. "Dude, haven't you heard?"

"What?" Bob stopped working over the pan. He could tell by the tone of Gary's voice that something was wrong.

Gary wiped his mouth with the back of his hand. "Dude, The Bitch is clearing out the labs."

"What's that mean?" Bob felt his chest tighten.

"Just a rumor, but I know someone who knows the vice president." Gary moved next to Bob and curved an arm over his shoulders. "All I know is, your lab's in the line of fire. I hope you don't get shot, dude."

"But—" The memory of Terri's departure at Cohen's hands settled on Bob. He struggled to catch his breath.

Jo Ann must have seen how devastated he was, because she slid over to put her arm around his waist. "You could call off the brunch. We'd understand."

Bob mumbled, "No, no, that's okay. You guys are here, and everything's almost ready." He circled the kitchen for a few minutes. His head popped up. "I've got some time now to make some banana bread for dessert."

He found the large mixing bowl and sloshed in all the ingredients. Dipping an electric mixer into the bowl, he beat the yolk of the eggs to splatter against the side. Increasing the speed of the mixer, he pummeled the ingredients. Shaking a handful of walnuts into the Cuisinart, he watched as the blades pulverized them. He ladled the contents into a baking pan and smacked the mixture with a spoon so hard it almost slopped over the sides as he shoved it into the oven. What about a tanning bed "accident"?

They all moved into the living room and kept drinking to get prepared for their nemesis.

An hour later, IT finally arrived. She paused at the door, waited until everyone had looked toward her, and walked in. Without looking at Bob, she shoved past him. From the center of the room, she announced, "I'm thirsty." Her breath smelled stale.

Bob fought to control himself as he thought about how much he wanted to kill her right on the spot. About how he could use the frying pan to bash her head senseless and how the chorizo and oil would fly all over, mixed with blood and bits of her brain. He stopped and took a deep breath.

Alone in the kitchen, Bob mixed a special margarita for Cohen. After pouring it into a stemmed glass, he washed out the shaker thoroughly. She grabbed the drink without thanks and slurped the opaque lime liquid. She ordered a second one from Bob, and they all waited, hungry, for almost an hour while she finished her drinks.

Then Bob cracked eggs into a frying pan, added the chorizo, salt and pepper, and turned the heat too high, almost burning the mixture. He set two eggs, crisp and brown around the edges, on top of a warm tortilla on each plate, and Jo Ann served them.

"Put the tomato chili sauce on top," Bob told them and turned to The Bitch. Staring at her, he said, "Hope it's not too hot for you." He didn't smile.

She grunted. "I love it hot, but my cardiologist told me to watch it. Seems I've got some new issues." She waited for anyone to console her. No one spoke.

During brunch, the conversation teetered from one topic to another, everyone careful not to mention work. For dessert, Bob returned from the kitchen with a brown loaf of banana bread. He set it directly in front of Cohen. "For you. A special recipe my grandma always made."

"I don't like dessert," Cohen said. She pushed the bread away. When she saw his expression, she growled, "Oh, for God's sake. You're always begging for something. Okay."

Holding a serrated bread knife to sever a slice off the loaf, Bob approached her from behind her neck. He glanced down and moved to the bread. He sawed off a slice and handed it to his boss.

She propped both elbows on the table and ate quickly. "It's okay, Bobby." Her breath wheezed, and she leaned forward to cough.

Bob watched her.

Cohen leaned back again, and Bob could see her throat working as if she couldn't swallow. "Are you okay?" Bob asked.

"Don't know." Cohen panted and rocked back and forth. A red flush rose from her chest to grab her neck. She stopped moving and sat straight up. She took a long drink of mineral water and said, "Better. Hope it's not the old heart." Cohen flashed a weak smile. No one said anything. "I think I'm okay."

Bob stared at her.

In a few minutes, the flush spread across her face. She tilted to the side. "Dizzy—"

Maureen jumped up, and her chair clattered onto the floor behind her. "Shouldn't we call 911? Someone?"

"Yeah," Gary agreed.

Maureen ran around the end of the table to stand beside Cohen but didn't touch her.

"My chest . . . can't breathe . . ." Her words slurred. "Aargh!" she screamed. Sweat spread across her face. It smelled metallic.

Maureen hopped from one foot to the other. "That does it. I'm calling." She ran into the bedroom, where she'd left her purse.

Bob remained on his side of the table. He watched as she fell off the chair and her body thudded onto the floor. Her legs quivered and her arms jerked to the sides. Then she rolled over onto her back and stared with red, unconscious eyes toward the ceiling.

A half hour later, after the emergency medics had done all they could for her, they told the stunned group she was dead.

"Heart attack?" Gary asked.

The older man shrugged. "Can't say. Could be."

"Will they do an autopsy?" Gary said.

"Maybe," the paramedic said. "Wait a minute. You say her name was Cohen? Was she Jewish?"

"She told us she had some heart issues," Jo Ann interrupted.

The group looked up from the body on the floor to Bob. He picked up three plates and Cohen's cocktail glass and washed them off thoroughly in the kitchen. When he returned, their eyes silently questioned him. He frowned and said, "Maybe it really was too hot." Bob grinned, but when he saw the gray faces around him, he stopped. He finally answered the medic, "Yes, she was Jewish."

"Okay." The man grunted as he reached across his knee into the black mesh bag on the floor. He removed a printed brochure. "New law just passed in Minnesota. Gotta give this to the next of kin. Do you know who that would be?"

"I can give it to her nephew," Jo Ann said. "Why?"

"See, most Muslims, Native Americans, and Jewish people object to any autopsy being done. So, this tells the family that they can object and we'll respect their religious preferences."

"Which means?" Bob leaned forward on one foot.

"The family probably won't want an autopsy," the older man said. He heaved himself up and wobbled on his front leg for an instant before he nodded to his assistant to bag the body.

Following are the first four chapter of Colin Nelson's newest book in the Pete Chandler series, *The Inca Code*. Chandler is an investigator for the U.S. Export/Import Bank. In this suspense mystery, he receives a cryptic message from an old friend in Ecuador begging for Pete's help. Before he can leave, the friend dies in a strange way—prompting Chandler to rush to Ecuador to solve the mystery of his friend's death. While there, Pete becomes the one whose life is threatened.

The Inca Code

Colin T. Nelson

Chapter One

How odd to receive a paper letter in the digital age, Pete Chandler thought as he opened the envelope. There wasn't any return address. A scratchy card fell out, and Pete turned it over. Handwritten in loopy letters it read:

Leftenant—
I'm outside the wire down here, and Ali Baba's on the perimeter. Send reinforcements!!

—Dow

Pete's stomach fluttered, and the chair he sat in felt hard against his back. It was from an old friend that Pete hadn't seen in years—Judd Crowe. Although they both worked for the U.S. Export/Import Bank, Pete was posted in Minneapolis, and Judd had gone somewhere in South America years ago.

Leaving his cubicle office at the bank, Pete hurried to an open area. He looked out the sixth floor window. Below him the Nicollet Mall was dotted with vegetable stands along the sidewalks. The sellers hid in the shadows of their tarps from the hot sun. Suffocating humidity still clung to the city—odd for this late in the summer. Customers on the street looked like hummingbirds darting from one stall to another before they hurried back to air-conditioned offices. Pete wore a cotton golf shirt, but dampness still spread over his chest. He took several deep breaths. What kind of trouble was Judd in?

He had been Pete's commanding officer in the Iraq war when they were assigned to the Army Criminal Investigation Command. More importantly, Judd had saved his life there.

Pete thought of him: short but solid as concrete, fearless and crazy. About fifty years old by now, and probably still married to

Deborah. Pete had been the best man at their wedding. If Judd needed Pete's help, it would be something serious.

He headed back to his office. Tan sheetrock walls at shoulder height gave him a little privacy. Pete had worked at the bank since leaving a disastrous investigative position in Washington, DC. Next to him the other investigator for the bank, Kendra Cooper, had a similar cubicle. Through the outside wall of his office, Pete heard people moving through the skyways that linked the buildings together with air-conditioned tubes of glass and steel. His boss, Martin Graves, had shoved the office in a deserted corner of the floor. Pete felt like he was on an island in a sea of open space.

Kendra stepped around the edge of the wall and rested her arm on the top. She wore bright yellow glasses that contrasted with her dark skin. "How's Ace Ventura, Pet Detective today?" she kidded him.

"Worried." He told her about the card.

"Crowe?" She cocked her hip to the left. "I met him once at a conference in Miami. Wicked smart, I thought."

Pete looked past her into open space. "Wonder what happened in South America?"

"Look him up. It's on the GF-OP 2000 site."

Pete leaned forward in his chair and stretched his arms. He was thin and in good shape, thanks to the tae kwon do training he practiced. "Great idea, but at my pay grade, I don't have clearance."

A smile crossed Kendra's face. "You can't do it, but maybe I can. I've got a contact at human resources in Washington. She owes me a favor."

Pete laughed. "After all, you're an investigator. I'd hate to be on the wrong side of you."

"Talk to my ex-husband. I took him down for max child support. Isn't hard if you know where to look for information and dirt." She straightened. Her lower half had filled out, but she always said her new man liked his women full-figured. Checking her smartphone, Kendra said, "Still got time. I can catch her now. Be right back." She turned and looped out of the cubicle.

In ten minutes, Kendra returned. "Here's the info on the dude." She set a laptop in front of Pete and pointed at the screen. Gold rings clustered between her knuckles, several on each finger. "I had my friend send it to my personal computer so it would be harder to trace if anyone got nosy."

"So much for tight government security. No wonder the Chinese can get access." Pete read the data on the screen to Kendra. "He's been posted to the Ex/Im Bank office in Quito, Ecuador, for eight years. Looks like he asked for the location specifically."

"That's unusual."

"Oh?"

"Well, the Ecuador/Peru office is only a tiny market for the bank. We've placed ten times more loans in Africa and India. Lot more action there." Kendra hummed a song as she sat in the only chair that could fit into the cubicle's space. "What was Judd's assignment?"

Pete continued to read. "He worked in IT. Looks like he was in charge of everything. I remember he loved cyberspace better than he liked the real space he lived in. Guy was desperate to get out of the Army and make some money. Big money." Pete ran his hand over his head as if to flatten his already combed hair. Black and still thick, it had receded up his forehead.

"Not going to happen at the Export/Import Bank. Thank God for our pensions." She leaned forward and pulled Judd's card from behind the laptop. "What's this mean?"

"I was a lieutenant, but he always called me 'Leftenant' as a joke between us. 'Ali Babas' was a term over there for the bad guys."

"And 'Dow'?"

Pete grinned for a moment. "Came from college, I guess. Judd took so many drugs that his friends called him 'Dow,' like the Dow Chemical company." When Kendra frowned, Pete continued, "By the time I knew him, he was totally straight. After all, he saved my life, and I owe him big time."

Images of South America dribbled into Pete's mind. Mountains, people wrapped in colorful blankets instead of coats, horses and guitars. Women with red lipstick leaning over iron balconies. And the sun glittering across the dusty domes of gray churches. What could possibly have threatened Judd there?

"Gonna go?" Kendra's voice interrupted his thoughts.

"I should."

"The bank's got some problems down there."

"Oh?"

"We're in a battle with the Chinese. The Ecuadorian and Peruvian governments are allies to the US, but lately they've hedged their bets and have actively sought Chinese financing for new projects."

"Maybe that's why Judd needs my help."

"Good luck, dude." Kendra grunted as she stood. "Not that you're asking, but if it were up to me, I'd go." She left a faint whiff of her musky perfume behind her.

Pete decided to heat some water for the instant coffee he always drank. He pulled out a packet of Via and ripped it open while the water boiled. Drinking instant coffee was a habit he must have gotten from his father, who had drunk it all his life. Not that Pete wanted to be like him. In fact, he tried in most ways to be opposite. The relationship between them had been rocky, to say the least. Pete still carried anger toward him that bubbled under the surface like the water in the pot on his credenza did now.

And the memories of his death, nine months earlier, still upset Pete.

Even more frustrating was that Pete had vowed to be a better parent than his father, but his relationship with his daughter, Karen, was also rocky. He was failing as a father just like his own parent had fallen short.

Part of the problem stemmed from the fact that Pete's blood mother was Vietnamese. His father had married her during the Vietnam War, brought her back to San Francisco, and then dumped her. He'd denied the heritage in Pete's life. Except for the darker tone of his skin and the slight slant of his eyes, Pete didn't look particularly Asian. Even so, it had been a source of bullying and teasing when he was growing up. When he turned to his father for help, Pete had received none.

The water boiled over, and Pete swirled the coffee into the cleanest cup he could find on the credenza. The water turned black without hesitation.

Judd had never asked for Pete's help since they'd been discharged from the Army. Pete decided to talk with the director of the office, Martin Graves.

On the tenth floor, Pete said hello to Graves' secretary. Graves had sufficiently high rank in the bank to qualify for a human secretary—called an Operational Adjutant. Pete stepped past the oak door and into the office. Because of the air conditioning budget cuts from Washington, the office was warm and sticky.

Graves looked up and waved Pete toward the circular table in the corner. Graves had pink skin and an expanding middle. He owed his position as the director of the bank to his unique ability to memorize government procedures and negotiate the Byzantine hallways of Washington. "What's wrong?"

"It shows, huh?" Pete sat at the table and crossed his arms over his chest.

"What is it?"

Although Pete trusted Graves, he was hesitant to tell him about the cryptic message in the letter. Graves didn't like to spend money on trips outside the bank's responsibilities. "How are the kids?"

Graves sighed. "Soccer practice started up again. Well, it never really ended. And with this heat, it's tough on the kids."

"Too bad you can't put a gin and tonic into a SuperAmerica coffee cup and sneak it onto the sidelines."

"Impossible. After months of games, we've become close to all the other families. They'd catch me." Graves led Pete to the table and pushed aside a half-eaten Egg McMuffin nestled among wrinkled paper on the table as if he were trying to hide it. It smelled of warm grease. "I know I've said it before, but thanks for the work you did in Southeast Asia. What a shock!"

"I couldn't believe it. The fallout has been bad, huh?"

"I'm sick at the thought of what the congressman did. And the God damned paperwork. Have you ever seen form GD 19567?

Twelve pages to fill out. Pain in the ass." Graves shifted in the chair, and the springs squeaked. "So, why are you here?"

Pete watched the glow of sunlight streaming through the window. Without looking at his boss, he asked, "Don't you have oversight for the Latin American offices?"

"Some of them." Graves nodded. "The western regions. Now that Colombia has stabilized, it's coming on as a new market for our lending."

"How about Ecuador and Peru?"

"Yes, those are also under my jurisdiction."

"Do you know the personnel down there?"

"Oswald Lempke is the director. Good man, smart, spent some time in our office here years ago."

Pete cleared his throat. From his back pocket, he removed the card from Judd Crowe and handed it to Graves. Pete said, "I want to go down there."

"After the trouble you had in Southeast Asia, I can't believe you'd ever want to go overseas again. And you know we barely survived the Republican budget onslaught in Congress this year. Funds are tight."

"I know, but look at that."

Graves read it. Pete interpreted the words for him. Graves remained motionless, shoulders hunched forward. His head bobbed up. "Wait a minute. I just got an e-mail from that office two days ago. Haven't opened it yet." Graves squeezed out of his chair and walked behind his desk. He tapped on the keyboard of his laptop. Without moving his head, he lifted his eyes over the top of the screen to look at Pete. In a scratchy voice, he said, "You better read this."

Pete hurried to Graves' desk and peered over his shoulder at the screen. Pete fell back a step, and his chest tightened.

The e-mail from the office in Quito read:

Memo, U.S. Ex/Im Bank, Quito, Ecuador, Avenida Cristobal Colon
From: Director Oswald Lempke

To: All personnel in grades E-3 and above

Message: It is with great sorrow that I inform you of the accidental death of our esteemed colleague, Judd Crowe. Judd was tasked with our IT for years and was a genius at his work. He will be missed by his wife, Deborah, and by all of his friends and colleagues here in Ecuador. More details to follow.

The air felt close and hot. Pete straightened and headed for the door. He took the space in a few steps and paused before leaving. "Get me a flight down there."

Graves called after him, "Don't forget to fill out form INT 989 before you go. It's my ass if you forget."

Chapter Two

By late afternoon, the Human Resources department at the Export-Import Bank had booked his flight through Miami and on to Quito, Ecuador. He'd leave tomorrow. People complained about "lazy government bureaucrats," but Pete found the people at the bank to be committed and hard working. The bank had been authorized by Congress during the Great Depression. Its mission was to lend in risky business situations in order to provide markets for American import and export opportunities.

On his way to Graves' office to check on the latest information, Pete's cell phone vibrated, and he read the text from his daughter, Karen. She would meet him at his place after dinner. His stomach tightened. He hoped it wouldn't lead to another fight. They'd made so much progress in their relationship up to now, and he wanted it to keep improving.

Pete found Graves reading his laptop. He curled his hand toward Pete to bring him closer. Graves stopped and said, "Well, the reports make his death sound kind of odd. Judd was on a tourist ride in a metal basket on steel cables over a river when he fell out of it." A smile squirreled across his mouth. "Of course, considering what I've heard about Judd's personality, I bet some exasperated tourist guide pushed him out." Graves stopped chuckling. "I'm sorry, Pete. I know he was your friend."

Pete raised his voice. "He saved my ass over there in more ways than I can say. And he was a great athlete. I'm surprised he fell out of anything."

"Okay. Problem is, no one actually saw him fall. The first thing anybody knew, a body was seen far below on the river bank. And his wife, Deborah, has already shipped his remains home."

Pete stepped around Graves' desk and read a summary of information from the Quito office. The more he learned, the more he wanted to go to Ecuador. He read out loud. "No autopsy done, cremated within twenty-four hours of death, local police aren't doing any investigation, and Deborah has already been to Judd's office to remove his personal things."

"That's fast."

"Too fast." Pete read more. "Judd was near a town called Baños, about seventy miles south of Quito."

"But no one saw him fall? Wouldn't you think he'd scream and draw attention?"

"Right. How could anyone miss that? Judd was wide as a brick." He continued to read. "Local police went down to recover the body. Our office was contacted and the body moved to Quito immediately." Pete ran his hand back over his hair.

"I want some answers," Graves demanded.

"I'm going to get them," Pete said and hurried out of the office.

He rode down the elevator and stepped onto the Nicollet Mall. The sun sliced between the high-rise office buildings and lit up the eastern side of the street in brushed gold colors. The heat and humidity hit him as he came through the revolving doors. Sweat popped out across his forehead, and he started across the street, closed to all traffic except buses. He felt like he was swimming through an aquarium that left a greasy coating on his skin.

As he headed for the parking lot where his car baked in the sun, he passed the old *Star Tribune* newspaper headquarters. Like so much of the media, it had changed, and now the office and printing plant crumbled before the wrecking crews.

The shell of the building still held broken floors and walls. Tangled steel rods twisted away from the wreckage. A man with a firehose sprayed the gray remains to keep the dust down. Beside him, two yellow excavators with long levered necks had buckets at the end that resembled open mouths. They poked among the wreckage like two T-rex dinosaurs browsing for food. When they found something worth eating, the jaws of the buckets darted forward, clamping down on broken sheetrock and cement, and tore off a big bite. Then, with a loud crash, they coughed their load into dump trucks that shuddered with the weight of the refuse.

The remains of the western wall blocked the sun and cast the work space in shadows. He could smell the dust.

Pete skirted past the site, but it left him with a sad feeling. His own life had pockets of wreckage in it. After the mother of Pete's daughter—they'd never married—had left him, he thought it was simply loneliness that shadowed him. It was, but there was more.

He'd been trying for years to improve the relationship with Karen. Things were getting better, but the gaps between them yawned open like the bucket heads on the excavators he'd just watched.

His office partner, Kendra, had suggested that he look deeper into himself to see if the difficulties came from him. How had Pete been parented?

She was right. As Pete thought back over his childhood and his father, Pete knew where the problem arose—not that he would blame his father for everything. Pete took responsibility, but the anger he felt at the bad parenting frustrated Pete and spilled over to his relationship with Karen. His inability to control himself made him as angry as the memory of his father.

He reached his car and got in to start it. He drove an old BMW convertible. Karen always kidded him that only old white guys drove those, but Pete didn't care. He loved the feel of driving with the top down. For a short time, he could pretend he was free of the wreckage that haunted him.

Pete slalomed through the typical Minnesota drivers, "speeding" along at forty-five miles an hour. He headed south. After reaching Highway 62, he looped off it to cross the Mississippi River by Fort Snelling and merged onto Shepard Road, which ran along a bluff high above another section of the Mississippi as it rushed toward downtown St. Paul.

After Pete had returned from Southeast Asia, he had only wanted solitude and peace. He'd almost been killed there trying to rescue someone. To escape from the stress of that experience, he'd bought a houseboat that was moored in the Watergate Marina on the river. For several miles, the banks of the Mississippi had been allowed to return to their natural state—much as they had probably looked hundreds of years earlier.

He reached the turnoff for the marina and waited while two bikers in bright red outfits pedaled by on the bike path that, like the river, ran into St. Paul. He turned and dropped down through the green tunnel that led to the water and the marina. The Crosby Farm Regional Park surrounded him with thick stands of oak trees that made Pete feel secure and sheltered in his houseboat at the marina.

He wanted some time to prepare for Karen's visit.

Her fiancé, Tim, had worked as a sous chef in a new restaurant called Ticket to Ride. Things had gone well for him. Karen and Tim had approached Pete shortly after he had returned from Myanmar. They wanted to buy into the restaurant. Pete was hesitant but agreed to fund part of the down payment. Business continued to grow, as did his relationship with his daughter. Pete had hoped this would continue. Then the problems started. Their best chef quit, suppliers couldn't get good quality chicken, and the cash flow dried up. Pete had a pretty good idea why Karen wanted to meet with him tonight. The thought made his stomach rumble again.

He parked on the gravel bank above the marina, put the top up, and walked around a steel box of wilted flowers at the head of the wooden gangplank that led down to the docks. Pete could smell the fresh water as it lapped against the boats. Down here, it even felt cooler. His houseboat was halfway out in the harbor at slip F-18.

He had electric and fresh water hook-ups that acted like an umbilical cord to keep him connected with civilization. Beyond that, when he shut the door of his boat, Pete was all alone, floating like an island on the swell of the water.

His houseboat was a Sumerset, and at forty-two feet, it was one of the smaller ones in the marina. Pete had sold his suburban home and bought the boat a year ago. He could stay there all year in spite of the water freezing because his boat had an aluminum hull strengthened with steel braces inside, designed to withstand the crush of ice.

Unlike older houseboats that looked like a boxy house set on a hull, his boat was designed to expose maximum open space. Each deck was positioned just ahead of the one below it, which made his boat look as if it were straining to go forward at high speed—

something that was impossible for a houseboat. And it was up to date with every gadget. He had navigation equipment that would enable him to cruise the Mississippi River as far as he wanted. A microwave, hot shower, depth finders, and even WiFi were included. He could be self-sufficient for months if he wanted to do so.

He remembered Judd Crowe. They'd met in officer's candidate school and became friends because they were both bored with the training. Judd always looked for angles to shortcut things—as he had with the training. Pete finished it as designed, but both of them were eventually commissioned and shipped out for the Middle East. Surprisingly, Judd didn't cut corners when it came to saving Pete's life.

The air conditioner hummed as it powered up and soon cooled and dried the interior. Pete changed into shorts and a t-shirt and put on his Keen sandals. He opened a Summit pale ale beer and made himself a bacon, lettuce, and tomato sandwich—even though it was too early to get authentic Minnesota tomatoes.

He went outside and climbed up to the top deck. He settled into a sling chair and finished his beer. The sun had dropped below the tree line to the west, so shadows crawled out from the regional park and surrounded the marina. Sound carried easily across the water. Pete heard the creak of boats around him, the quiet murmur of people, and the chugging of air conditioners. Outside the shelter of the marina the Mississippi rushed along in silent power. In contrast to the lush green of the shoreline, two white gulls swooped across the marina, probably looking for food as they always did.

The year-round boat community was insular, but Pete was starting to make friends. What he liked about them was they had purposely rejected the typical lifestyle of most other people: suburban homes, expensive downtown condos, and mansions near golf courses. Like them, Pete felt he didn't fit anywhere else.

He looked at his watch. Karen and Tim would arrive soon. Pete thought of Karen's mother. She'd left Pete, saying that he "brought her down." That came from a line in a popular rock tune of the times—probably as deep as she was capable of thinking. Still, she was one of many women in his life who'd left him or he'd been forced to leave. He pushed the thoughts from his mind. Not a great way to prepare for meeting Karen.

This time, he'd remain calm and try to understand what she needed. Just the opposite of what his father had given Pete. He recalled a time in grade school when he'd been teased a lot because of his Asian heritage. Coming home, he expected his father to support and maybe even defend him. Instead, the old man had ignored the issue, and Pete realized his father was embarrassed about it and didn't care much about how Pete felt. Funny how those childhood traumas still carried so much power in adult lives.

Pete looked up to see Karen's Prius turn into the marina parking lot. She parked and walked across the lot with Tim at her side. Karen led by a step and moved with a purposefulness that Pete admired. Like him, she was assertive and didn't let people push her around. Maybe that created some of the problems between them: they were both strong-willed people.

When she lifted her head, she waved at Pete. A breeze blew her black hair to the side, and Pete could, for an instant, recognize the Asian roots in her face.

She took a skip and started down the gangplank. When they came alongside on the dock, Pete called down from the top deck, "Welcome aboard."

"Hey, Dad." Karen wiped off her sandals on the dock and stepped over the gunwale onto the deck of the boat. Tim followed.

Pete hugged Karen and smelled fresh shampoo in her hair. He shook Tim's hand. "Want to come in or sit on the deck?"

Karen waved her hand in front of her face. "Let's go in. I've been in the kitchen all day at the restaurant. I want cold air." She followed Pete inside the cabin. He offered each of them a beer, which they accepted. They moved from the galley to the salon and sat. Pete took the wooden deck chair. Brown tinted windows kept the glare of the sun out and left them in a soft darkness.

"How was your day?" Karen asked him.

"I'm going to South America. Ecuador."

Her forehead wrinkled. "Leaving again? Seems like you just got back from Myanmar."

"An old friend of mine died there. I want to help his wife if I can. Besides, you know me. I'm an investigator; I'd like to see how Judd died. Something about his death doesn't seem right to me."

"Make sure you get your hair cut before you go," she warned.

"Huh?"

"It's too long; makes you look old." She looked out the window twice, crossed her legs, and said, "Uh, Dad. I guess we should talk about the restaurant, huh?"

A knot formed in Pete's stomach, but he forced himself to breathe slowly. "How are things going?"

Karen hesitated, then turned to Tim. "We're still leaking cash," he said. "We've got a deadline at the end of this month. We're behind on the mortgage payments, and if we don't come up with the balance owing, we lose everything."

"I thought you cut your overhead." Pete's voice took on an edge that he didn't intend.

"Of course," Karen said. "But the costs just keep climbing."

Pete stood and took a drink from his beer to slow down his racing thoughts. Then he asked, "So, how much money are we talking about?"

"Uh, fifteen thousand."

"That's a lot. Have you checked with your parents, Tim?"

He twirled one of his dreadlocks between his fingers. "Already talked to them. They've helped as much as they can."

Pete looked out the window at the docks and watched as people walked by, pushing plastic carts filled with groceries. He turned back to them. "I don't know."

"We'd pay you back," Karen said.

"I already gave you ten thousand after I got back. I don't want to—"

"I hate doing this, Dad. You know that, but we're desperate."

"I want to help, but I can't keep bailing you out. I never got any help from my father."

"Oh, drop the pity party," Karen shouted. "So your dad was a creep. You don't want to be the same, do you?"

That hit him hard, right in the chest at about heart level. He hated the thought of being like his father, of being a terrible parent, of not helping, but just throwing money at the kids wouldn't help either. Pete worried the restaurant was a losing effort anyway, no matter how much money was pumped into it. He spoke each word carefully. "No, I don't want to be like him. But I also think being a good parent means I don't rescue you every time you ask."

"But this is an emergency," Karen said.

"I know," Pete said to stall them.

"Oh." Karen raised both arms and slapped them down along her sides. "You told me what happened in Southeast Asia and how you learned that Asian people help each other, more than Americans ever do. Well, we're of Asian heritage—or are you still repressing that, too?"

"I don't want to talk about it now." A passing cruiser moved behind the stern, and Pete could hear the engines gurgle as it passed.

"You never want to talk about it," Karen said. "That's the problem. You deny your heritage because of your anger with your father. Now's the chance to get that stuff behind you. Let's work together to help Tim and me."

While Pete tried to answer her, she shouted again, "Because your problems are hurting us. I'm sorry Grandpa died, but it's not fair to take it out on us."

"I have to think about it." Pete squeezed between them and slid open the glass door that led to the deck. He walked to the stern and climbed up to the second deck. A hot breeze came off the river.

Five minutes later, he came down and entered the salon. Karen and Tim sat in the dusky interior in silence. Pete said, "Okay. I'm leaving for Ecuador tomorrow. I need some time to think about it. Can't promise anything." He knew it was the coward's way: leave the country to avoid having to make a decision right now. Would this cause the relationship with Karen to fail? Pete couldn't predict, but by going to Ecuador, at least he wouldn't fail Judd.

She took a deep breath and stood up, almost as tall as him. "I was hoping we wouldn't fight about this. We've been getting along so much better."

"I agree." He looked her in the eyes. "But our relationship shouldn't be dictated by money."

"Of course not, but this is our life." When he didn't respond, she continued, "So, have a safe trip to Ecuador. How long will you be gone?"

Pete ran his hand over his hair. "Just a few days, probably."

There were a few minutes of awkward silence until Tim moved toward the sliding door. He opened it and stepped through. Karen followed him, and Pete hurried behind her. She gave the door a strong shove, and it struck Pete in the forehead. It hurt like hell, and a gusher of blood erupted from his head.

"Oh, Dad. I'm so sorry," Karen wailed.

Tim rushed back into the galley and found a towel on the granite counter. He handed it to Pete, who pressed it to his forehead. Soon the towel was soaked with blood. "Let's get you to an emergency room," Tim said.

Pete nodded, as he could sense how serious the injury was. He picked up another towel from the kitchen and followed them out to the dock and their car. The pain pulsating from his head matched the pain in his heart. This was a hell of a way to end the conversation with his child.

Chapter Three

Pete waited at the Minneapolis/St. Paul International Airport for his flight to Miami and then to Quito. Above his left eye, a large bandage itched where it covered the six stitches he'd received at the emergency room. A blue bruise streaked across his forehead and made him look like he was a veteran of the Iraq war.

Maybe it was a good thing to be leaving right now. His life was littered with wreckage here in Minnesota. It would be good to take a break and have time to think about Karen's request for more money. And his father's death still bothered Pete more than he'd expected it would.

His plan was simple: meet with Judd's wife, try to comfort her, and do a quick investigation of his death. In a foreign country he'd be hampered in that investigation, but he'd meet with the director of the Export-Import Bank in Quito, Oswald Lempke. Maybe he'd have contacts with local police who might be willing to help in Pete's mission.

He left Minneapolis, arrived in Miami, and left again for Quito for a flight of less than five hours. He learned the country was in a similar time zone, which would eliminate any jet lag and make his work easier for the short time he'd be in Ecuador.

As usual, the bank had provided Pete with extensive research about the country, which he scanned during the flights. Named Ecuador because it straddled the equator, it was about the size of Colorado but held an incredible amount of diversity. It had world-class wildlife and geography that included the Andes Mountains, some of the highest active volcanoes in the world, steamy Amazon jungles, and a long Pacific coastline of beaches and fishing villages that looked out to the fabled Galapagos Islands six hundred miles offshore. It attracted a diverse group of outdoor tourists and adventurers and, increasingly, American retirees looking for a pleasant climate and cheap living.

The country had been stable for years. Huge reserves of oil and natural gas in the Amazon had driven the economy to allow the government of President Rafael Correa to pour money into infrastructure like schools, roads, and social security programs. He'd done that by defaulting on the nation's debt, renegotiating oil contracts to Ecuador's advantage, tightening the tax system on the rich, and turning to China for new loans. The government had also taken steps to create new industries, anticipating the time when the oil and gas would eventually run out.

Pete's jet dropped down through dense clouds that obscured the ground. The plane approached the Mariscal Sucre International Airport twenty-two miles outside of Quito. Once past the clouds, Pete could see snow-capped mountains and volcanoes, some smoking with twisting plumes of gray, ringing the valley of the city. The sides sloped down into dark, hidden valleys. As the plane banked into its final descent, the sun blinked off the snow in a flash of pure white.

The city was draped over a high plateau, and it looked from above like someone had spilled a chocolate malt. Cocoa-colored fingers dripped into the valleys between the volcanoes. As he got closer, Pete could make out shapes in the tan mass: boxy houses painted in pale colors of ochre, yellow, burnt sienna, and even blue. They stacked against each other up the hillsides in higgledy-piggledy confusion. Gray steeples of tired churches poked above terra cotta roofs that gave the top side of the city a bumpy, orange look.

After landing and clearing customs, Pete worked his way through the immaculate airport. The first thing that struck him was the altitude. Although he had taken some meds to help, at 9,350 feet above sea level, Quito was the highest capital in the world, and Pete felt it. He stopped walking to catch his breath. He felt tired.

Advertising on the walls reminded him of the ancient Incan empire that had existed here. The research from the bank recounted how the Incas had spread, through war, from Peru into Ecuador in the 1400s to reach as far north as Quito. The Incas forced the indigenous people to adopt their language, *quechua*, and to worship the sun. Some of their sun temples still existed in the valley around the city.

By 1534 the Spanish conquistador Francisco Pizarro had conquered Peru, and his generals moved north to Quito. After hard fighting, the Spanish overran Quito and within fifteen years controlled most of what is modern Ecuador. They called it the Royal District of Quito. About two thousand Spaniards had subjugated about half a million indigenous people and, in the process, killed tens of thousands of the locals.

As he rode through the narrow streets of Quito in a taxi, Pete saw the continuing struggle of various religious beliefs from the past: magnificent cathedrals and monasteries squeezed next to shops offering the services of local shamans or healers who still spoke the Incan language and worshipped both the sun, *Inti*, and mother earth, *Pachamama*.

The healers were known as *yachacs*. Pete had learned that they practiced an ancient combination of superstition, myths, and the belief that the volcanoes were powerful entities because they were associated with earthquakes, eruptions, and thunder.

The cab exited the Avenida Libertador Simón Bolívar and turned into the city. Pete marveled at the capital. It was the best preserved colonial city in South America.

The cab driver spoke good English and introduced himself as José, the "friendliest driver in Ecuador." He had learned the language from the American nuns who taught at his school. Pete chatted with him, asking about the sights passing by the windows.

José changed the subject as they passed an American chain hotel, the Marriott. "We like Americans here," he said. "We use American dollar as our currency, *cómo no?*"

"Right."

"Many years ago your oil companies rape environment, and we were mad at you. Now they are more careful, but we have new enemy."

"Who's that?" Pete leaned forward over the seat.

José turned down the pan pipe music on the radio. Serious talk was coming. "Chinese. They are taking over country. Our president and government are still corrupt."

Pete had seen corruption all over the world in his work for the bank. Unfortunately, it was a common problem that crippled many countries and hurt the local people. "What do you mean?"

"President Correa turned his back on many traditional markets and lenders. Instead, he loaded our country, like a burro, with billions of dollars in debt owed to the Chinese. It is based on future oil sales, and now Chinese are involved in many oil and mineral companies."

"I suppose you worry about oil for the future."

"*Claro,* because the supply of oil in the ground is limited, of course." José glanced in the rearview mirror and cleared his throat. "I believe Chinese *puercos*, or pigs, will do anything to make money. They are all crooks."

Pete shrugged his shoulders in agreement.

José squinted into the mirror. "Are you Chinese?"

Pete's eyes jerked up to meet José's. "No, why do you ask?"

"I can tell you have Asian blood. I hope you not Chinese."

The driver annoyed him. Pete quit talking and looked out the window. Memories of the bullying he'd experienced as a child came back. Although he didn't look particularly Asian, people knew, and kids had made fun of him because of it. Pete was more annoyed because he'd let a cab driver trigger the bad memories. "Can you just get me to my friend's house?" He snapped off the words.

Pete had called Deborah Crowe from the airport and agreed to meet at her apartment in Quito on the north side, where many of the diplomatic, business, and wealthier people lived.

When he arrived at the white stucco house, Pete got out and paid José five dollars but didn't tip him. Pete walked up a cobble-stone sidewalk to the wooden door. He lifted an iron knocker and heard a boom echo from within. Bougainvillea cascaded over the tiled roof, splashing pink and red flowers everywhere. They grew around a wrought iron lamp hanging at an odd angle next to the door.

Deborah opened the door, and her eyes softened when she saw Pete. They fell into each other's arms and hugged before speaking.

He remembered to always call her Deborah, as she insisted, never Deb or Debbie.

She stepped back into the cool interior, and Pete looked at her. He hadn't seen her or Judd for years. She stood, angled slightly to the left, a small woman who always dressed perfectly. Deborah looked great as usual. Her eyes were large but not red or puffy. Maybe she'd cried everything out days ago, even though Judd had only been gone for less than a week.

"Thank you so much for coming, Pete." Her voice was controlled and low. "Judd would've been pleased."

His throat felt tight for a moment, and he couldn't speak. Then he croaked, "I owe him so much. He saved my butt in the Middle East."

She glanced at his forehead. "What happened? Is the banking industry getting that violent?"

He tried to laugh it off. "An accidental meeting with a sliding door. Does it look that bad?"

"Lots of black and blue." Deborah reached for his hand, held it in her own dry hand, and led him through the entryway into a low-ceilinged living room. That gave way to an open terrace enclosed by a waist-high wall painted in whitewash. A blue awning sheltered the area from the sun. Pete gazed across the valley, the city of Quito, and up the other side to see the Rucu Pichincha volcano. He took a deep breath while he looked around at the stunning scene. The air was so clear it seemed like he could see for miles. Puffy clouds hung motionless around the mountains as if the clouds had been snagged on the peaks when they tried to pass by.

A Celestron Nexstar telescope tilted up at the sky in the corner of the terrace. Pete commented on it.

"Judd was an amateur astronomer. I never paid much attention to what he did, but I know he spent a fortune on that." Deborah offered him a chair in the far corner next to a low table. A huge vase cradling a bunch of red and white roses took up most of the surface. "Flowers are one of the biggest exports to North America from here. The bank has lent to many of the start-up companies. Since I

love flowers, that's one of the few things I'll miss when I leave."
Each flower was three and a half inches in diameter.

Pete could smell their sweetness in the air. "Don't you like it here?"

Deborah sniffed and turned her head. "Oh, it's okay. It's clean, and the people are friendly, but there is a huge mixing of the races. *Mestizos.* You'll see the Indian influence all over: short, dark people with sharp noses. And their eyes are set close together." She laughed and looked at Pete. "You'll stick out like a sore thumb—tall, thin, and built like a wide receiver."

"Oh." He sat in a tan sling chair. The leather felt warm from the sun.

Her eyes opened wider. "But don't be fooled. The whites still run everything."

Pete felt uncomfortable with the subject. He changed it. "Things seemed to have moved so quickly after Judd's death. When are you leaving?"

"In a couple hours." As if to explain, she added, "I want to get back to Minneapolis with Judd's ashes and take care of them."

Pete sat up, surprised at her haste. "It must be difficult for you."

"I just want to get the hell out of here." Deborah cocked her head to the side briefly. She didn't look at him. "Now where is that damn *quechua*?" When she turned back, Deborah must have seen the question on Pete's face. "We call these indigenous people *quechuas*. It's the ancient Incan language they all speak among themselves when they don't want us *gringos* to know what the hell they're doing behind our backs." When she turned her head again, her blonde hair, cut at chin length, flipped around in the opposite direction. Deborah shouted into the living room, "Martita. Where is the tea?"

She turned back to Pete and sat in a chair at an angle to him. Bare legs stretched from her skirt and ended in high-heeled shoes. Pete wondered if she dressed this formally all the time.

"It's so beautiful here. Did Judd like it?"

Deborah shrugged. "Some parts of it. He always said it was a great place to do business."

"Oh?"

Deborah's eyes shifted back and forth as if she were revealing something important in a crowded room. "The government is relatively corrupt, and if you know the right people—well, you can get anything done. Don't tell Martin Graves about that."

"He's been around. He probably knows anyway." Pete looked up as a small, dark woman in a bright yellow dress came onto the terrace with a silver tray. She squeezed two china cups and a pot on the table next to the flower vase. Without a word to Deborah, the woman left.

"Coca tea. Made from real coca leaves—the same ones used to make cocaine—eventually." Deborah smiled. "This is a common form drunk by everyone to help combat the effects of the altitude. Even after I acclimatized, the thin air still affects me. Here, this will help you." She poured a saffron-colored stream into the cup and handed it to Pete. "Be sure to drink plenty of liquids, avoid alcohol for a while, and go for the carbs at meals," she advised him. She looked at her watch.

The tea tasted slightly bitter, like herbal tea. "I know this may be difficult for you, but I'm also here to check on Judd's death. Some things seem odd to me."

Deborah waved her hand in front of her chest. "Nothing odd about it. He's gone. Too bad, but life goes on."

"Of course, but I'm curious about a few of the details. I'm an investigator, after all. Part of my personality," he said.

"Oh, it's very simple, really. He fell. Luckily the local police got there quickly. They helped me get his body back to the city." Her words tumbled out fast, as if they were too many to be held in her mouth.

"May I ask why he was cremated?" Pete probed carefully. The tea must have been helping, as the slight headache he'd felt had drained away.

She looked out across the valley. Her hands massaged the teacup in her lap. "Judd's request."

"Can you tell me where the mortuary is?"

"Oh, I can't remember—" She hesitated. "Oh yes, it's called *Descansa Tranquila*, Peaceful Rest."

"What about the details of Judd's death? How did he fall? I remember him as a great athlete."

She answered quickly, "I was on the tour with him, but we'd separated so I could shop for alpaca blankets. Consequently, I didn't actually see what happened. There's a tourist ride across the Rio Verde. It's a steel basket that people stand in while it travels across a deep valley toward a waterfall on the far side. He fell out of the basket."

"Anyone in the basket with him?"

Her voice hardened. "Like I said, I wasn't there. I don't know any more."

Pete sat forward in his chair. "What was he working on at the bank?"

"He loved the techie stuff. He maintained all the bank's computers, wrote new software. He was an expert." She glanced at her watch again. "I'm worried the taxi to the airport will be late. The people in this country can't even read a clock."

"I also have an appointment tomorrow to talk with Oswald Lempke. Do you know him well?"

"The 'Wizard of Oz'? I didn't know him well; Judd did, of course. Lempke seems to be able to perform magic at times." She twisted around and yelled for the maid. "These *quechuas*, you can't depend on any of them. The pot's gone cold. Where the hell is she?"

"I don't remember, but do you have any children, Deborah?"

"No. We tried for years but gave up eventually."

Pete tried to catch her eyes, but she kept looking away. Was it grief or something else? He told Deborah about the card Judd had sent. "Was someone mad at him? Sometimes he could rub people the wrong way."

She stopped moving. "No, I don't know what you're talking about."

"He said there were bad guys after him."

She shrugged but didn't say anything more.

Pete paused to think about a tactful way to ask the next question. "I know Judd always wanted to get rich. Could his problem have been something about money?"

A pink blush washed over her face for a moment. Her eyes found his and she said, "So, that's why you're really here. It's all about money. I don't think you give a damn about my husband's death, do you?"

Pete back-pedaled. He hadn't expected this reaction. "Uh, it's only part of why I'm here. The home office is concerned—"

"Are they going to try and screw me out of his pension?"

"No. You know Judd was my friend. I'm trying to find out what happened to him."

Deborah's cup clattered onto the table, and she jerked out of the chair. "I'm disappointed, Pete. I thought more of you."

He stood also. "You've got this wrong."

"No, I've got it right." She started to walk toward the living room. "I have packing left to do before my flight this afternoon. Maybe you should go." She stopped and said over her shoulder, "And do your *investigation* somewhere else."

Pete hesitated, trying to decide if there was anything he could say to clear up the misunderstanding. He followed Deborah to the front door. She swung it open, and a breeze out of the valley blew through from the terrace. Without the warmth of the sun, it felt chilly. Pete turned to face her. "Deborah—"

"Good-bye." Her eyes pushed him backward and out the door onto the cobblestone walkway.

Pete walked to the street. *What caused that?* he wondered. *Grief? Stress?* Even with all his investigative skills, had he totally screwed up?

Within a block he found a taxi with four numbers on the side —an official one. He ducked into the back seat and negotiated a fare before the driver put the car in gear. Pete was about to give the address for his hotel when he changed his mind. "Do you know where the Descansa Tranquila funeral home is?"

"Descansa Tranquila?" The driver shook his head. Then he leaned over to the glove compartment and retrieved a smartphone. His finger crawled across the screen like an ant looking for food. His head popped up, and he smiled with dirty teeth. "*Sí, sí, por supeusto.*" He drove around the corner and headed up a hill. With the exception of the original main plaza—the only large, flat space in the city

—Quito crawled over the foothills of the surrounding mountains and volcanoes. Roads always twisted around the contours, up and down throughout the uneven city.

They headed up a narrow street only wide enough to let the taxi squeeze through. People edged along the sides, and the taxi missed them by inches. The car bumped over the cobblestones.

Within twenty minutes, the driver stopped in front of a one-story building. Papers blew across the sidewalk, and two dogs lay in the sun next to the door of the funeral home. A neon sign read: Descansa Tranquila. The double wooden doors looked heavy and were both open.

Pete motioned the driver to wait, and he stepped over the broken concrete sidewalk to go inside. The interior was dark and cool. Wood paneling lined the walls up to waist height. At the end of the hall, an iron cross with a figure of Jesus on it hung from the ceiling. He seemed to bless a man sitting below at a low desk that had carvings of flowers on the legs. The man looked up from a laptop computer. He had shiny black hair, white skin, and drooping eyebrows that looked like collapsed tent walls next to his eyes.

"*Bueno, Señor. Cómo estás?*" He stood.

When Pete asked him if he spoke English, the man nodded, and Pete said, "I understand that an American friend of mine was cremated here a few days ago."

The man smiled. "That is—"

"His name was Judd Crowe, and his wife's name is Deborah. I believe the police brought his body here after he died in an accident. The remains have already been sent back to the States."

"That is correct. I received the body." When he turned to look at the computer screen, a flash of light reflected off an ear stud, and Pete saw the tendrils of a blue tattoo disappear down his neck into his collar. "It is unusual to cremate a body in my country. The police brought in the deceased, and the wife identified him, insisted on the immediate cremation, and wanted the remains shipped to the US as soon as possible. Everything was so rushed. In her exact words, she wanted to 'get the hell back to America.'" The man snorted quietly and continued, "I do not think she likes our country."

Pete rubbed his hand over his head as if he were flattening the hair. "Thanks." He turned to leave and looked back. "Tell me, was she upset, crying?"

"Crying?"

"Yeah. Her husband had just died."

"I did not pay attention. But when she paid the entire fee in cash, I looked at her. I remember she was not crying."

Chapter Four

The next morning at the NH Royal Quito Hotel, Pete tried to reach Deborah Crowe on her cell phone. She didn't answer and must have already left the country. He hurried into the dining room for breakfast. Most of the hotels in Latin America offered a full breakfast to guests. Although he was anxious to find out what had happened to Judd, Pete was tempted by the food.

Scrambled eggs, stuffed tamales, potatoes, pancakes for the North American guests, and bowls of fresh fruit from the Amazon crowded the long table. He drank coffee with milk.

Pete hoped that a meeting with the director of the bank in Quito, Oswald Lempke, would answer his questions.

He walked through the lobby toward the floor-to-ceiling windows that looked out to the Avenida 12 de Octubre. While the concierge called a cab, Pete stepped outside. Warm sun flowed around him like water, and he looked down the street toward the main part of the city below. Orange-tiled roofs cobbled against each other for as far as Pete could see. A woman walked by wearing a pink shawl with a baby wrapped in a blanket slung over her shoulder. Her skirt was rainbow colored and dragged on the ground. A wool snap-brim hat perched low over her eyes.

The driver arrived, and Pete told him the address of the bank's office on Avenida Cristóbal Colón near the main plaza. Tires crunched over gravel as the taxi merged into the busy street. He turned right and moved onto a four-lane road with a boulevard dividing two lanes on either side. They passed a one-story colonial building with a sign that read Embassy of Paraguay. Under arched loggia, four baskets of dying flowers hung in the sun.

The driver reached a roundabout and curved to the right, and Pete saw a statue of Abraham Lincoln sitting in a small park of dried grass in the center of the circle. Four blocks later, he saw a statue of Winston Churchill. He asked the driver about them.

"Those are gifts to the city from the Americans and the British. We never turn down anything free here." He laughed and squirted through a break in the heavy traffic. Buses lumbered alongside the cab, belching diesel exhaust.

The taxi stopped in front of an old colonial building two blocks from the main plaza on the Avenida Cristóbal Colón. At one time, the building must have boasted a brilliant white marble façade, but now it looked gray, its corners crumbling. He entered through carved wooden doors. Some signs of affluence still remained: the brass door handles gleamed in the sun, the red tile floor looked expensive, a large stone fountain in the courtyard burbled with water, and pink lilies floated in the pool. The courtyard was open to the sky, and Pete could see the sun peeking over the eastern edge of the roof to light up the row of curved arches that led around the second floor of offices. In the shadows behind the arches, doors remained closed.

He walked down the hall. His steps echoed against the stucco walls. Pete came to a broad stone stairway. The steps were low, and as he climbed to the second floor, Pete felt the effects of the altitude again. When he reached the top, he was panting.

At this level the signs of financial accomplishment were even greater: wooden floors had been polished, potted palms stood guard before every mahogany door, and beside each one a gold sign boasted of the tycoons who hid within. Pete reached a double door with a sign that read *Export/Import Bank of the United States of America. Please ring for admittance.*

He pushed the button under the sign. When he heard a faint buzz, he opened the right-hand door, stepped inside, and knew immediately he was on American turf. A painting of a cabin on a lake surrounded by woods and a large framed photo of Manhattan hung on the walls.

An Ecuadorian woman came from the back room, heels clicking across the floor, and smiled at Pete. She extended her hand.

"Welcome to the bank. Are you Pete Chandler?" Her hair was thick, shiny black, and pulled into a tight bun behind her head.

"Yes. Is Mr. Lempke in?"

"He's expecting you. Follow me. Would you like some of our excellent coffee?"

"Uh, do you have any of that coca tea? I still feel kind of light-headed."

The woman chuckled to show perfect teeth that looked even whiter against her chocolate-colored skin. "Of course. It takes a while to acclimatize." She led him down a narrow hallway to a large office in the corner. Pete followed her inside and saw a man dwarfed behind an immense desk. Probably because of the high altitude, his office felt chilly and dry. In the corner fireplace, flames wiggled above burning logs.

Lempke looked up at them and rose immediately. "Chandler? Welcome to Quito." Lempke came around the desk, shook Pete's hand, and pointed to a huge stuffed chair. Pete lowered himself into its depths. He smelled leather, and it surrounded him like a luxurious cocoon. Lempke sat on the opposite side.

"How was your trip?" Lempke asked. He wore wire-rimmed glasses with photo-gray lenses. They must have been old because the lenses hadn't completely cleared, so Pete had difficulty seeing Lempke's eyes.

"It was fine. I came because of Judd Crowe's death. He was a close friend of mine."

"Unfortunate business," Lemkpe said. "One of our best men here at the bank. A real genius with computers and tech issues."

"Did he work in this office?"

"No. We have a satellite office farther from the plaza. Cheaper rent, you know." Lempke spoke softly, with a slight lisp, and enunciated every word. "How's my old friend, Martin Graves?"

"He's fine." Pete wanted to get on to the questions that bothered him about Judd's death, but he found the conversation with Lempke was comforting in an odd way. Although he'd never met Lempke before, there was something familiar about him. "I understand you lived in Minneapolis?"

"On and off, for many years. I'm originally from the East Coast. Worked at the bank in Washington and was transferred to the Twin Cities. I loved it there."

"I've also worked all over the world in various security positions."

Lempke straightened his body in the chair. "Say, by any chance are you related to Frank Chandler?"

Pete's chest twitched. "He. . . he was my father."

Lempke smiled. "Thought so. I can see the resemblance."

"Oh?"

"Well, I mean from your mother's side."

Pete's breath came hard. From the altitude or his surprise at the new information? "How do you—?"

Lempke smiled. "Your father came to the bank years ago. As I recall, he had a steel manufacturing business, and he was looking for financing. Can't remember if we ever gave him the money or not. And I remember your blood mother was Vietnamese. It was common during the war."

"My father never mentioned anything about you, even though he knew I worked at the bank."

"A reserved man, as I recall. Maybe he kept his business to himself." Lempke nodded in agreement with himself.

Pete didn't want to think about his father, but the revelations dredged up memories. To say his father had been "reserved" was an understatement. His father was isolated and never talked to Pete. The only time he did was when he was mad at Pete. There was an incident at dinner when his father had become furious at something and challenged Pete to fight him. He had forced Pete into the garage and actually started to swing his fists. Another example of great parenting.

"Pete? You okay?"

"Sure."

Lempke leaned forward and said in a soft voice, "Still getting over his death, huh?"

"Yeah, I guess so."

"I did some checking on you. Don't worry, I had problems with my old man. I was removed from my parents when I was quite young. Raised in foster homes. My advice—just forget about him. You don't need anyone, believe me. I've achieved success with my own efforts."

Pete wondered how the conversation had morphed into this subject. "Uh, I didn't come here to talk about my problems. Let's talk about Judd."

Lempke sat back in the chair. The receptionist came into the room carrying two cups. She set one of coffee before Lempke and a cup of *mate de coca* tea in front of Pete. He drank it quickly.

"What can you tell me about his death?" Pete asked.

"I don't know much about it. Local police handled everything. Judd had gone to a town called Baños, which is famous for eco-tourism. Unusual for a tourist attraction, but he was alone on the ride—a basket that ran on cables across a deep gorge. Somehow, he fell when he was over the river. It rains a lot down there and it's foggy, so things could've been slippery."

"Any witnesses?"

Lempke's head twisted back and forth once. "There was an operator; maybe he saw it happen. And the local police were more concerned about getting emergency help to Judd at the bottom. They failed to interview anyone else."

"What? I can't believe that."

"Each town has a small police department and not much more. Many of them are corrupt and incompetent anyway. In terms of law enforcement, Ecuador is far behind what we expect in America."

"What kind of work was Judd doing for the bank?"

"As you know, we lend for risky investment opportunities that private banks wouldn't touch. Judd was in charge of all our computer data services, from loan reviews to compliance issues."

The lenses on his glasses had cleared, and Pete could see sharp blue eyes behind Lempke's pointed nose. "Why was he in Baños?"

"He'd gone on vacation with Deborah. It's a popular spot for outdoor activities. Didn't you serve with Judd in Iraq?"

Pete's head tilted back. "We served in the Criminal Investigation Command. Went through OTC together and got to be good friends. He loved to break the rules, and I liked that about him. But when it came to our duties, he was all business."

"I understand he saved your life."

"Right. We were interrogating an Ali Baba that we thought had been cleaned off—I mean, had been frisked for weapons. When I turned my back on him, he jumped me and put a knife to my neck. He started sawing away until Judd reacted, pulled out his .45 automatic, and shot him."

The fire hissed in the corner while a log cracked in half.

Pete pulled out the card Judd had sent him. "Does this make any sense to you? Any idea why someone should be threatening him?"

"No. Of course, I don't involve myself in our employees' personal lives. Judd had an unfortunate habit of offending people, if you know what I mean."

"I do."

Lempke looked away. He glanced at a crossword puzzle that rested on the arm of his chair. He must have been working on it before Pete arrived. "Anything else I can do to help you?" Lempke said.

"I was hoping for some answers about his death."

Lempke shrugged. "An unfortunate accident. A good man who was steady and did his job. That's all."

That didn't sound like the crazy Judd Crowe Pete had known. "I'd like to look at the scene." He felt embarrassed to keep pushing. "I'm an investigator, after all."

"I suppose you can. I'll get a driver from the bank to take you down to Baños." Lempke glanced at his watch and stood. "It's been a pleasure to meet you, Pete. Keep in touch through my secretary." He turned to walk back to his desk.

Pete watched him and suddenly understood why Lempke looked familiar. His hair was the same color as Pete's father's hair. Dark red, almost brown, with a balding spot on the crown, as his father's hair had had.

Pete hurried toward the door. Lempke's secretary almost bumped into him.

"Agent Silvio Castillo is waiting to see you, sir. Remember, he's here to talk about Mr. Crowe?"

Pete stopped. "Who's Agent Castillo?" He whirled around to face Lempke. "What's this about?"

"I don't know," Lempke said.

"If you don't mind, I'll stay."

"Uh, sure." He waved at his secretary. "Show him in, Consuela."

She brought back a tall man dressed in an expensive, double-breasted suit. He was dark skinned with straight black hair, silvered along the temples. He removed a white Panama hat and placed it on the arm of the chair Pete had just vacated. Castillo's posture was military, and he gripped each man's hand. "Thank you for meeting me, Director." He spoke excellent English. "One of your employees, Mr. Judd Crowe, has come to our attention. I am investigating about some concerns we have."

Lempke responded, "Unfortunately, Mr. Crowe died a few days ago. An accident when he fell into a deep river valley."

Castillo frowned and dropped his head for a moment. Then he continued, "Yes, I'm aware of that, and it troubles me greatly."

"It also troubles us," Lempke said with a lisp. "He was a good and loyal employee of the bank."

Castillo cleared his throat and shifted to stand on his other leg. "I work for the Secretariat for Multidimensional Security in this region. It was established in 2005 to increase our law enforcement ability across borders. Traditionally, in Latin America we have relied on local police. In today's international climate of crime, that's not adequate." He pulled out a leather notebook from inside his suit coat. On the cover was a hand-painted copy of the Mona Lisa. Castillo opened it and flattened a page.

Pete stood up. What did this have to do with Judd? he wondered. It didn't sound good.

"I'm curious. What does your job include?"

Turning to Pete, Castillo said, "We handle broad defense and security issues, terrorism, drug trafficking, infrastructure protection, and cyber security."

"That's all?" Pete tried to joke, but no one else laughed.

A brief smile creased Castillo's lips. "Tourism security also." He closed the notebook. "And who are you?"

Pete introduced himself and explained why he was there.

"You came all the way down here for an accident?"

Pete felt his back stiffen. "Yes, yes I did. You might not understand the friendship I had with Mr. Crowe."

"This sounds suspicious to me." Lopez took a step forward. "Are you looking for the money also?"

"What the hell are you talking about? No. I've got my own reasons to be here, and they're none of your business, by the way."

Lempke sliced his hand down through the space between Pete and Castillo. "All right. That's enough. The last thing we need to do is fight. We all want the same thing."

Castillo looked out from under his dark forehead. "I'm not sure we do." He glanced at Pete but continued, "Mr. Crowe is at the center of our investigation."

"What do you mean?" Lempke asked. "I hardly think he was a terrorist."

"No, I don't think he was," Castillo said. "But we were contacted a year ago by your Treasury Department, specifically their Global Illicit Financial Team, in relation to a company he ran."

"A company he ran?" Lempke's face flushed red. "What the hell are you talking about?" His words tumbled out. "Mr. Crowe was the chief IT supervisor for the Export/Import Bank of the United States here in Quito."

Castillo said, "Yes, but perhaps he ran it secretly. It is called the Dow Cyber-Security Corporation." When neither Lempke nor Pete responded, Castillo continued, "It contracted with major companies to protect their computer systems."

"What?" Lempke stammered.

Pete smiled to himself when he heard the name. Same old Judd with his crazy sense of humor. "Who were his customers?"

Castillo tapped his finger on the notebook. "I do not know extent of his business yet. It's one reason I'm here to talk with you. Development is booming across Ecuador and Peru. Perhaps he wanted to 'get in on the ground floor,' as you Americans say, in the security business."

"Well, even if he had this company, what's wrong about that?" Lempke crossed his arms over his chest.

"It's more complicated." Castillo removed a computer printout from the inside pocket of his suit coat. He walked over to Lempke's desk. "On my own authority, I will share this with you." When the director nodded, Castillo unfolded the paper and smoothed it with his palm. He set the notebook with Mona Lisa's face next to it. "Look at these transactions."

Pete stood on one side of Castillo while Lempke moved to the other side. Pete read a series of entries:

Pay to account: U885673-2: 170,000 NS
Pay to account: U347884-3: 340,000 NS
Pay to account: U347884-3: 275,000 $
Pay to account: U556900-7: 850,000 NS

"What's it mean?" Lempke said.

Castillo stood back. "These are recorded transfers of money. NS means *nuevo sols*, the Peruvian currency. With the present exchange rates, we estimate this represents a total of at least 675,000 in American dollars."

Lempke's face flushed pink. "So, what the hell does this have to do with Mr. Crowe?"

"These are bank transfers representing investors' money going into his accounts for the Dow Cyber-Security Corporation. There could be many more, but these are the initial results from our investigation."

"Still doesn't mean a damn thing." Lempke shuffled backward into the office. "I'm mad as hell that he didn't inform me, but starting a company isn't a crime. You're wasting your time."

"How were you able to get this information?" Pete asked.

"The Secretariat has broad powers of investigation." Castillo smiled. "But then, this is South America. Through my family and friends, I have additional contacts at the highest levels in both countries. Unlike your country, we are not tied by ridiculous laws of privacy. I can get whatever information I need."

Lempke turned. "So why are you here?"

"I had hoped to talk with Mr. Crowe, but since he died, I thought you may have further information about his activities."

"Well, I don't, and frankly, it's none of your goddamn business as far as the bank is concerned."

"You make him sound like a criminal," Pete said.

"Maybe this will help you understand our concerns. There is a prominent Chinese businessman here in Quito. His name is Xiong Lo."

At the mention of the name, Lempke snorted, "I know him. Shady. What the hell do you want with him?"

Castillo lowered his voice. "In our preliminary scan of Dow Cyber-Security Corporation records, Mr. Lo came up as one of the largest investors. I don't know what is going on, but his presence makes me suspicious."

"Damn," Lempke said. "Here at the bank, we wouldn't touch him with a ten-foot pole." When Castillo frowned, Lempke explained, "American idiom. We don't trust him."

"Why would Mr. Crowe deal with someone like Lo?" Castillo spoke slowly and let the words dangle in the air.

"To make money," Pete insisted. "He always wanted to get rich."

"Yes, I can understand that. But where did all the money go?" Castillo spooned out the words for Pete to follow.

"Huh?"

"Besides the deposits into Mr. Crowe's accounts I showed you, other records indicate he withdrew almost as much cash in the past two months." Castillo looked from one man to the other. "There has been a huge increase in investments from the Chinese into our economy. Much of the inflow is for illegal activities. What you call 'money laundering.'"

"Wait a minute." Pete's voice rose. "I fought with this guy in the Middle East. I'd trust him with my life." Anger threatened to overwhelm him. From bad experiences in the past, Pete tried to keep it in check. But Castillo had already charged and convicted

Pete's friend. If Judd were alive, he'd already be locked up in a damp South American jail cell and probably hanging by his thumbs.

Oswald Lempke paced to the large window behind his desk, filled with small panes of glass pieced together in a lead frame. He stared outside at clouds crossing the sky.

Castillo folded the printout into a small square and replaced it inside his jacket. "I'd like the cooperation of you and the bank to help us. I assume I could receive it?"

Without saying anything, Lempke nodded his head.

Pete was so shocked that he couldn't talk for a moment. He sensed Castillo would leave soon, so Pete said, "I'm sure we'll find out Judd was completely clean." He didn't trust Castillo, but he obviously had resources and information that Pete could use. "I'll be happy to work with you."

"Good."

Pete ran his hand back over his hair, even though it was in place. "By the way, what is it with all of you and the Chinese here? Even my cab driver hates 'em."

"You may as well learn this now," Lempke spoke up. "We're in a war with Chinese competition for investments around the world. In Africa, for instance, their export/import bank has increased lending by eight-fold in less than ten years. They're also trying to buy up everything here." He sneered, "This is the new cold war, and I plan to win it."

Castillo handed a white card to Pete. "Contact me there." He picked up the leather notebook and cradled it against his chest. Pete commented on it.

Castillo held it out to show Pete. "This represents civilization and all that humans have accomplished. I have all my case notes in here. If I lose this, it could mean the fall of civilization."

Pete studied him closely.

A smile cracked between Castillo's lips. "Maybe I should say that if I lose this, I'm afraid we'll lose the progress we've made in South America to combat crime. I look forward to solving this mystery." Putting on the Panama hat, Castillo tugged at the brim to settle it on his head.

"Let's be honest, Señor Castillo," Lempke said. "I'm sure your investigation will be above-board, but how are you going to deal with the corruption here?"

Castillo's face hardened, and he didn't respond for a moment. "I have my own reasons for solving this. Corruption—that is life here. But I assure you I can handle that problem in my own way."

"Like the 'Untouchables,'" Pete said. When it was obvious Castillo didn't understand, Pete continued, "Too bad we can't talk to Judd to clear up this mess, but with the accident—"

Castillo waved his hand in front of his chest and leaned close to Pete's face. Castillo said, "Don't forget the bigger problem we face now: where did the money go, and what was he doing?"